A PLUME BOOK

CLOUDS WITHOUT RAIN

Calais Photography

PAUL LOUIS GAUS lives with his wife, Madonna, in Wooster, Ohio, just a few miles north of Holmes County, where the world's largest and most varied settlement of Amish and Mennonite people is found. His knowledge of the culture of the "Plain People" stems from more than thirty years of extensive exploration of the narrow blacktop roads and lesser gravel lanes of this pastoral community, which includes several dozen sects of Anabaptists living closely among the so-called English or Yankee non-Amish people of the county. Paul lectures widely about the Amish people he has met and about the lifestyles, culture, and religion of this remarkable community of Christian pacifists. He can be found online at: www.plgaus .com. He also maintains a Web presence with Mystery Writers of America: www.mysterywriters.org.

CLOUDS
WITHOUT RAIN

AN AMISH-COUNTRY MYSTERY

P. L. GAUS

A PLUME BOOK

PLUME
Published by the Penguin Group
Penguin Group (USA) Inc., 375 Hudson Street, New York, New York 10014, U.S.A. •
Penguin Group (Canada), 90 Eglinton Avenue East, Suite 700, Toronto, Ontario, Canada
M4P 2Y3 (a division of Pearson Penguin Canada Inc.) • Penguin Books Ltd., 80 Strand,
London WC2R 0RL, England • Penguin Ireland, 25 St. Stephen's Green, Dublin 2, Ireland
(a division of Penguin Books Ltd.) • Penguin Group (Australia), 250 Camberwell Road,
Camberwell, Victoria 3124, Australia (a division of Pearson Australia Group Pty. Ltd.) •
Penguin Books India Pvt. Ltd., 11 Community Centre, Panchsheel Park, New Delhi – 110 017,
India • Penguin Group (NZ), 67 Apollo Drive, Rosedale, North Shore 0632, New Zealand
(a division of Pearson New Zealand Ltd.) • Penguin Books (South Africa) (Pty.) Ltd.,
24 Sturdee Avenue, Rosebank, Johannesburg 2196, South Africa

Penguin Books Ltd., Registered Offices: 80 Strand, London WC2R 0RL, England

Published by Plume, a member of Penguin Group (USA) Inc. Reprinted by arrangement
with Ohio University Press.

First Plume Printing, December 2010
10   9   8   7   6   5   4   3   2   1

 REGISTERED TRADEMARK—MARCA REGISTRADA

The Library of Congress has catalogued the Ohio University Press edition as follows:

Gaus, Paul L.
    Clouds without rain : an Ohio Amish mystery / P. L. Gaus.
        p.   cm.
        ISBN 0-8214-1379-1 (cloth : alk. paper) — ISBN 0-8214-1380-5
(pbk.: alk. paper)
        ISBN 978-0-452-29668-8 (pbk.)
        1. Amish Country (Ohio)—Fiction.   2. Amish—Fiction.   3. Ohio—Fiction.
I. Title

    PS3557.A957 C58 2001
    813'.54—dc21

                                                        00-054536

Printed in the United States of America

PUBLISHER'S NOTE
This is a work of fiction. Names, characters, places, and incidents are either the product
of the author's imagination or are used fictitiously, and any resemblance to actual persons,
living or dead, business establishments, events, or locales is entirely coincidental.

Because of my wife, Madonna,
and dedicated to our daughters,
Laura and Amy

Jude 12

These men are blemishes at your love feasts, eating
with you without the slightest qualm—shepherds
who feed only themselves. They are clouds without rain, blown along by the wind; autumn trees,
without fruit and uprooted—twice dead.

Thursday, July 6, 2000
Associated Press

For the first time in at least 20 years, the average
price of farmland in Ohio exceeds that of all the
other Corn Belt states. The steady development
of houses and shopping centers in rural Ohio
eventually pushed the state into the top spot, an
agricultural expert said yesterday. "In the past,
farmland was owned by farmers for agricultural
purposes," said Allan Lines, an agricultural econo-
mist at Ohio State University. "What we're seeing
now is we have all these other interests there in
owning a piece of the real estate."

Preface and
Acknowledgments

Not all of the places in this story are real, but all are as authentic to Holmes County, Ohio, as I know how to make them. Any resemblance to persons living or dead is purely coincidental, and any reference to legal and trust practices is my own fabrication, as are the events in this story. I have moved and altered the description of the psychiatric ward at Aultman Hospital. The ritual barn was located in Panther Hollow, not Walnut Creek Township. It has been destroyed.

Thanks go to the excellent staff at the burn unit in the Children's Hospital Medical Center in Akron, Ohio, especially Julianne Klein, RN, BSN, and Mary Mondozzi, RN, MSN, as well as to Mark A. Harper of the Akron Fire Department, Ed Gasbarre of R. W. Gasbarre and Associates, Inc., surveyors, and Dr. Wayne M. Weaver of the Joel Pomerene Memorial Hospital in Millersburg.

Many thanks to Amish and former-Amish friends who do not wish to be named, and also to Chief Steve Thornton, Tom Kimmins, Esq., Ray and Kaye Fonte, Pastor Dean Troyer, and Eli Troyer—good friends, able advisors.

1

Monday, August 7
4:15 P.M.

PROFESSOR Michael Branden, driving a black Amish buggy, worked his horse at a walk along Walnut Creek Township Lane T-414, just north of Indian Trail Creek in Holmes County, Ohio, on a sweltering Monday afternoon early in August. Coming up to one of the short stretches of blacktop laid in front of a house to cut the dust, he slowed the horse and rolled gently onto the pavement. The buggy rocked and swayed from side to side on its light oval springs, and the iron wheels cut sharp lines through the tar blisters in the blacktop. The horse's hooves gave hollow plopping sounds that switched back to a lighter clicking in the dust and gravel after the blacktop played out beyond the house. The sky was cloudless, the sun hot, and beyond the thin line of trees that bordered the lane, the fields seemed withered and spent, the crops stricken with thirst.

Branden was dressed to outward appearance as an Amishman. The Amish clothes and broad-brimmed straw hat with a flat crown were his own, bought two summers before, when he had worked on a kidnapping case involving an Amish child. He was wearing shiny blue denim trousers over leather work boots, a dark blue shirt with the sleeves rolled up to his elbows, and a black cloth vest, unfastened in front.

Under his vest, he had hooked a deputy sheriff's wallet badge over the belt he wore instead of the traditional suspenders, a concession to English style so that the heavy badge and three pairs of handcuffs would ride securely at his waist. The belt also held a beeper, though locating a phone in those parts of the county would be a task.

The professor brought the rig to a stop, took off his straw hat, poured a little water from a plastic bottle over his wavy brown hair, and rubbed at it vigorously. Then he laid his hat on the seat, and while he dried his tanned face and neck with a red bandanna, he straightened the rest of the gear riding beside him.

There was a black radio handset from the sheriff's department, turned off for the task at hand. A Holmes County map from the county engineer's office, folded to the square of Walnut Creek Township. An elaborate Contax RTS III SLR camera with a long Zeiss lens, tucked securely into the corner of the buggy seat. On the floorboards under the seat, a Smith and Wesson Model 60 .357 Magnum revolver in a black leather holster.

With a light slap of the reins, Branden started the horse again. About a hundred yards further up the lane, he pulled into the drive of a new two-story Amish house and stepped the horse to a stone watering trough. A door on the upper floor opened as he stopped. Lydia Shetler, dressed in a plain, dark-blue dress and black bonnet, came out onto the top porch of the house and asked, "Any luck, already?" with the classic Dutch accent of the region.

The professor shook his head and said, "Mind if I water the horse?"

Lydia intoned, "If it suits you," and leaned over with her elbows on the porch rail to watch.

The porch, braced with tall posts, was level with the second floor of the house. The area under this high porch was latticed in front with a rose arbor, which made a shady breezeway at ground level. The family's laundry was hung out for the day, drying on clotheslines in the breezeway.

Branden climbed out, and as the horse snorted and drank water, Lydia asked, "How much longer do you figure to make these rides, yet, Herr Professor?"

"Till we get them," Branden said and laughed. He slapped his hat at the dust on his ankles and added, "Or until the sheriff gets bored with the idea."

Lydia nodded as if to say that she understood the sheriff's impulsiveness well enough, and asked, "Are you sure only our two families know about your business?"

"Why? Have you heard anything on the gossip mill?"

"Not a word."

"Then I suppose I'll still keep riding. As long as nobody at either end lets it slip."

"I haven't heard any mention," Lydia repeated, and went back inside. Branden mounted into the buggy, swung around on the wide gravel lane, and walked his horse out to T-414 again, continuing east toward the little burg of Trail.

This was his fifth afternoon drive in two weeks, traveling the northern edges of Walnut Creek Township on the center-east edge of Holmes County. His assignment was to be the decoy in Sheriff Bruce Robertson's strategy to catch the two Amish-clad teenagers who were making a reputation for themselves that summer by robbing the Peaceful Ones. Disguised in rubber goat's-head masks, they rode up to the slow-moving buggies on their mountain bikes and demanded money. Surprisingly large sums had been involved, and Sheriff Robertson now had his decoy in place. Professor Michael Branden, Civil War History, Millersburg College, a duly sworn reserve deputy, with a buggy, a costume of Amish clothes, a radio, an ample supply of handcuffs, and a very expensive camera. Also a revolver, just in case.

As the professor rattled along slowly in his buggy, a pickup shot by in the opposing lane. In the cloud of dust left in its wake, two Amish teenagers passed from behind on mountain bikes. Branden took up his camera and fired off several frames on motor drive.

Branden tensed a bit, wondering what he would actually do if the young bandits ever did approach him demanding money. He wasn't at all certain that the sheriff was right about this one. Amish or English, they wouldn't be that easy to apprehend. "They're Amish, Mike," Robertson had said. "They'll just stand there when you show them your badge." And if he took their picture or stepped down from the buggy to confront them? What then? They'd take off on their bikes.

That'd be it, Branden thought dourly. They'd scatter, and he wouldn't have a chance of chasing them down in the heat. The professor shook his head, laughed halfheartedly, and wondered about the ribbing he'd take from the regular deputies if the sheriff's little game should play out as he suspected it might, with him giving chase through fields or over hills, losing them both.

Chagrined, Branden rode the rest of his shift haphazardly back and forth along narrow T-414, radio off so as not to give him away. As the supper hour approached, he headed south on T-412 to return the buggy to its owner. As he brought the buggy into the Hershbergers' drive, one of the middle sons, Ben, stepped out of a woodshop at the side of the property, slapping sawdust off his long denim apron. He waved to Branden and came down the steps to a hitching rail beside the gravel drive. The drive curved gently around a well-tended volleyball court and dropped with the slope of the land into a wide valley, passing the north side of a weathered white house. Three stories and gabled, the historic building had a round sitting room and cone-shaped roof set at the corner, where a large covered porch began at the front and wrapped around the side. Grandmother Hershberger sat peacefully in an oak rocker on the elevated porch, a small mound of potatoes on the floor at her side, peeling long, curling skins into her lap. Branden tipped his hat, and she glanced briefly at him with reserved acknowledgment. As Ben came forward and took the horse by the bridle, Branden turned on his handset radio and heard Sheriff Bruce Robertson shouting, "Two ambulances. Maybe three! Ellie, send five!"

"Fire's on their way, Sheriff," Ellie Troyer said, her voice frayed with tension.

"It's a mess, Ellie," Robertson's voice cracked staccato over the radio. "One buggy, maybe more. Can't tell yet. A semi jack-knifed. Cab upside down in the ditch. The trailer has taken out at least one car and it's burning now," followed by, "For crying out loud, Ellie, where are my squads?"

"On their way," Ellie said, managing to sound calm.

"Schrauzer's unit is up there right in the middle of the whole thing," Robertson shouted into the microphone. "Can't see him anywhere. Going closer, Ellie. Get those fire trucks down here NOW!"

The mic clicked off for a bit and then Robertson called in again, more subdued. "Get the coroner, too, Ellie."

Branden pulled his buggy up sharply, set the hand brake, scrambled down onto the driveway, and took the radio off the buggy seat. He paced in a circle on the drive as he made his call. "This is Mike Branden. Over."

Ellie's voice came back. "Signal 39."

"Township 412 at the Hershbergers." As he spoke, he gathered his things from the buggy and walked quickly to his small pickup.

"It's right there, Professor," Ellie said. "You're practically on top of it. 515 south of Trail."

"Roger that," Branden said and started his engine. "515 south of Trail. Ellie, I'll be right there!"

He pulled the door closed, fish-tailed on the gravel lane, waved at Ben, and heard Robertson come over the radio.

"Mike, you come in from the north. South of Trail. That'll put you on the other side. I'm farther south, the other side of the pileup, and I need someone on your side to stop traffic."

"I'm coming up on Trail now," Branden said, steering with his left hand, holding the handset with the right.

"Turn right at Trail, Mike," Robertson said. "Slow. We're down in a little valley and if you don't come in slow, you'll run us all over."

Branden dropped south out of Trail on 515, came around a sharp curve and over a hill, and saw a tall plume of black smoke beyond the next rise in the road. He came up to the top of the hill, stopped abruptly, stepped out of the truck, and leaned forward on the open door, shaken by what he saw some hundred yards below.

A semitrailer rig sprawled across the road, the cab overturned in the right-hand ditch, the trailer laid across the road on its side, its rear wheels spinning slowly over the left-hand ditch. The truck driver lay twisted on the pavement beside the overturned cab.

A monstrous gasoline fire engulfed a sedan pinned under the far side of the trailer, and dense smoke drifted up and trailed west over a field of stunted corn. The flames leaped from the road to the grasses in the roadside ditches and spread rapidly into the withered crops in the fields on each side of the road. Even at this distance from the wreckage, Branden could smell the smoke and the gasoline. He heard a car approaching behind him and turned to stop it with a palm held outward. A second car pulled up, and then a third. He took up a position to block the passing lane and turned back to view the wreckage.

Just beyond the burning sedan was Phil Schrauzer's cruiser. Something long and bulky had punched through the windshield. Further back there was a line of two pickups and a produce truck, all apparently uninvolved in the wreck. Two of the three drivers stood helplessly beside their trucks. The third had stooped to open a briefcase on the pavement. As Branden watched, the man took a cell phone out of the briefcase, stood sweating profusely while he dialed a number, and talked as he turned his head this way and that, looking with astonishment at the wreckage that lay around him. The man fixed his gaze on the house at the end of the driveway, spoke for a moment longer, switched off the cell phone, and dialed another call. He spoke for perhaps a minute, listened briefly, and tossed the phone into the briefcase on the pavement. Kneeling down, he closed the case, and stood to drop it through the open window onto the front seat of his pickup.

The sheriff's black-and-white 4x4 was stopped in the passing lane beside the produce truck, door hanging ajar. Another sheriff's unit was parked at the top of the next hill, turning cars back toward Walnut Creek. A cruiser from the state highway patrol came past the roadblock and pulled in behind Robertson's 4x4.

Branden stepped over to his pickup, reached in under the seat, pulled out binoculars, and turned the dial back to a full wide-angle view. He turned momentarily to check on the line of cars and trucks that had stacked up behind him and saw that his roadblock was self-regulating, as some cars turned back to find another route.

When he first held the binoculars to his eyes, black smoke filled the eyepiece. He trained right and found the bottom of the overturned cab, its front wheels hanging awkwardly in the air, the driver motionless on the ground. He moved the binoculars up and left and found Robertson waving the state trooper closer to the fire.

Robertson pushed toward the fire with his forearm over his eyes and reached Deputy Schrauzer's cruiser. Branden cringed as he saw the sheriff start to work at whatever had pierced the windshield, struggling to pull it back out with his left hand, while he tried to steady Schrauzer with his right hand through the driver's-side window.

The fire in front of Robertson flared violently, and Branden, startled by the massive orange fireball, sucked in air through his teeth and stumbled backward. There was a shattering crack of glass as flames expanded out and upward. Robertson turned his back and bent low beside the cruiser, shielding himself from the flames. But after a few seconds the big sheriff lumbered up onto the hood of the cruiser, and the trooper dashed up to take charge of Schrauzer, still pinned in his seat. As writhing gasoline flames spread toward Robertson, the sheriff pulled what looked like a tight bundle of wooden poles out of the windshield. He tossed it onto the pavement beside the cruiser and climbed down from the hood. Shirt ablaze, he helped the trooper drag Schrauzer out of the cruiser and along the pavement, away from the flames. Once Schrauzer was clear, Robertson threw himself onto his back and rolled from side to side, while the trooper beat at the flames with his hat.

There was another flare-up over the burning car, and Branden heard the first squad's sirens out on the high Walnut Creek hill. The ambulance crested the hill, sped into the valley, and went directly past the trucks to where Robertson and the trooper crouched beside Schrauzer, who was laid out on his back.

Branden watched as the highway patrolman began to help Robertson out of his uniform shirt, still smoldering. Robertson bent suddenly backward and appeared to cry out in pain as the shirt stuck to the skin on his back. A paramedic hurried forward and cut the shirt loose from patches that had fused to ugly burns on the sheriff's skin. Nancy Blain, in jeans and a T-shirt, stood back from the sheriff, snapping photos for the *Holmes Gazette*.

A team of paramedics loaded Schrauzer into an ambulance and headed back toward Millersburg. Robertson turned and surveyed the crash scene, as a paramedic from a second squad tended burns on the sheriff's back and arms.

Branden watched Robertson, bare-chested, directing fire department volunteers to the burning car, with pieces of his uniform shirt clinging to his back. The sheriff took a step toward the fire, and the paramedic pulled him back by the arm. Gratefully, Branden sensed that Robertson then seemed content to stand back and let the squads do their jobs.

The first fire truck to arrive had started laying foam on the burning car. Nancy Blain darted here and there among the wreckage, taking photos with her black Nikon. Up on the hill behind the wreck, the professor trained his binoculars on the ground at Robertson's feet, then in wider circles on the ground in front of the semi. In every direction on the opposing hill, both on the pavement where Robertson stood, and sprayed over the vehicles and terrain not directly damaged by the impact of the crash, Branden saw a vast scattering of black fabric and wooden splinters. Back up the hill there lay a thin axle. Smashed and twisted buggy wheels lay in the ditch beyond, two of them still attached to a second bent axle. The largest fragment of the buggy lay in the field at the edge of the road, some twenty yards away from the cab of the semi. In its tangled mass, Branden made out the torn and twisted fabric of Amish attire. Nancy Blain's slender figure came into view, as she aimed her camera at the buggy. She lingered for several shots there and then stood and began firing off frame after frame as she pivoted full circle in place.

A second pumper arrived on the scene. Having extinguished the fires at the car, the firefighters ran their heavy hoses out into the burning fields and sprayed a broad arc of water on the outlying ridges of fire burning through the crops. Branden looked again for Robertson, and found him kneeling beside the road, near the overturned cab of the truck.

He was holding the head of the downed horse by its bridle. The horse's back legs had been mauled by the impact, and the right hind leg was torn loose at the hip. The horse's coat was matted with blood and its flesh was ripped open, exposing the bowels. The front legs of the horse pawed uselessly at the air. Branden saw Robertson draw his sidearm and point it at the head of the horse. There was a puff of smoke at the muzzle, followed abruptly by the report of the gun, and the horse lay immediately still.

2

PASTOR Cal Troyer crested a hill on a gravel lane south of Walnut Creek and turned left into a crushed stone driveway, where a two-story white frame house with a green roof stood in the lee of a mature stand of blue spruce mixed with wide oak and tall hickory. He parked his old gray truck off to the right of the drive, where a small patch of gravel normally was occupied by a buggy. Out of the barn to his right, two teenage boys drove a pair of draft horses hitched to a manure spreader, waved briefly, and turned toward the field beyond the trees.

On the lawn at the side door, Cal greeted two small children, a boy and a girl, about four or five years old, splashing in full Amish garb in a round plastic toddler's pool. They stopped when he spoke to them, but, obedient to their teaching, they did not reply.

He stepped up onto the small porch, rapped his knuckles on a wooden screened door, and was admitted by a young girl in a long purple dress and a white cap, who let him in and kneeled immediately to sweep a small mound of dust into a dustpan on the gray wooden floor. Behind her, the floor into the kitchen was bright and clean, and before Cal took another step, she caught him gently by the sleeve, produced a weak smile, and pointed to his shoes. Cal nodded, untied his white cross trainers, and slipped his feet out of them, saying, "Is Andy Weaver staying here?"

The girl stood up with her dustpan and broom, said, "For a spell," and pointed the end of her broom handle toward a door on the other side of the kitchen. She had never met Cal Troyer, but recognized him from stories of his long, white hair. Like everyone in her community, she knew of the preacher's reputation as a friend to her people. She stood respectfully and studied his powerful arms and large carpenter's hands. He thanked her in a gentle voice and stepped over his shoes.

In the kitchen, uncomfortably warm from the wood stove, a mountain of rising dough nearly two feet abreast and a foot high lay on the open door to the oven. In a corner behind an icebox, another daughter was scrubbing the floor with a damp towel wrapped around a pine two-by-two board, switching from one side of the board to another as each became soiled.

Cal asked again for Andy Weaver, and the teenager said, "On the back porch."

Cal pushed through the heavy walnut door the first girl had indicated and entered a large dining room with several china cupboards and a round dinner table with ten chairs and one highchair. The only other door in this room led to a moderately sized sewing room, where three women—eldest daughter, grandmother, and mother, Cal guessed—sat leaning over a square wooden quilting frame. As they took small stitches in the ornate patchwork of cloth, only the mother looked up from her work.

Cal asked, "Andy Weaver?" and she wordlessly nodded toward a screened door behind her.

The door led Cal to a long concrete walkway connecting a Daadihaus to the main house, and on the porch of the little house, Cal found Bishop Andy R. Weaver sitting on a three-legged stool, mending tack, or rather holding it in one hand while he gazed, lost in thought, at a distant fence line.

Weaver's hair was pushed down over his ears by a battered straw hat. His shirt was dark blue, and his trousers were of denim. His long gray beard fell loose and uncombed on his chest, and he was shaved around the mouth, though some stubble was evident.

"Andy," Cal said, and approached. Weaver turned, saw Cal, and rose to offer his hand happily, saying, "You're white, Cal," indicating Troyer's shoulder-length hair and full beard.

"Been a long time, Andy," Cal said. He shook his old friend's hand and added, "So it's *Bishop* Andy, now."

Weaver nodded self-consciously and said, "Thought I had gone to Pennsylvania for keeps, Cal. Take a walk?"

Cal retrieved his shoes, and the two strolled through a swinging iron gate and along a rusted fence bordering a sunbaked field of hay. The bishop's old straw hat was broken open at the front of the crown where he had pinched it so often, putting it on and taking it off. His vest hung limply over rounded shoulders. The leather of his boots was split and scuffed, encrusted with patches of dried manure.

Cal drew a pair of sunglasses from his shirt pocket and put them on. After they had walked a ways, he said, "What made you decide to come home, Andy?"

Weaver stopped, stuck his thumbs in his suspenders, and studied his boots. He kicked at some dirt, looked at Cal somewhat ambiguously and said, "They've all promised to change."

"And your brother?"

"So, you remember."

Cal nodded and Weaver said, "He's been out for a long time, now."

"Bishop Yoder kicked him out?"

"Should have," Weaver said, passing judgment.

Cal's fingers toyed with his long white beard. He stood thinking silently in the bright sun about the old days, about the crusade against cults that he and Weaver had organized some years ago. After a moment, Cal shook loose from his memories and asked, "They're all going back to Old Order?"

Weaver shrugged unhappily. "Not all. I lost one family already."

"I doubt you'll lose that many more."

"The rest are waiting to see how I'll rule on various things."

"They asked you back to help after Yoder died?"

"The most of them did. A few holdouts, I suppose," Weaver said.

"But you're bishop now. They'll align themselves under your authority."

"People here have gotten too far along into modern ways, Cal. Getting back to Old Order will be hard."

"They all knew you well enough before you quit for Pennsylvania. Wouldn't have asked you back if they didn't mostly want Old Order."

"You don't know how far gone Yoder let the District get."

Cal reached down, plucked some dry alfalfa, and stuck it between his teeth, waiting for Weaver to continue.

"Think about it, Cal. We've got at least three neighborhood phone booths out by the roadsides where no one person can be said to actually own the things. Some have secret phones in their barns, and I can't tell you how many have cell phones tucked under pillows. I've even got two families who own vans. They each hire drivers, but they still own the vehicles, for crying out loud."

"They'll get rid of it all, if you tell them to."

"The old ways are disappearing, Cal. It's the kids more than anything. They won't have farms the way things are going. Right now, there are at least nineteen of them working in shops or stores. Some restaurants, too. For as long as six years in some cases. They're not going to be able to farm. Probably not marry in any traditional way, either."

"Shops seem to be the way to go, these days," Cal offered.

"They've got too much idle time on their hands," Weaver complained.

"Are you going to go to the sheriff with those other bishops? About the drinking parties?"

"The sheriff can't stop our young people from drinking, Cal."

"It'd be a start," Cal offered.

Weaver shook his head soberly. "It's the cult, Cal. After all these years, it's still that cult."

Cal nodded, cast his eyes at the ground, and kicked up dust angrily, remembering the problems he had faced in his own congregation, when the thing had first gotten started. He and Andy Weaver had crusaded against it throughout the county. In the end, all they could do was to expose it, and keep their own people from mixing in. After that, Andy had moved away, Cal had tended to his own congregation, and the cult had grown quietly to the point where it seemed that everyone in Holmes County knew about it, without feeling the need, in these more liberal times, to stand against it. Live and let live, is what they all would say. Who's to judge, anyway?

"I judge it," Cal thought to himself, and looked back sternly at Weaver. Revulsion for the cult sank deep furrows into his brow.

Andy peered into Cal's narrowed eyes, laid a hand on his shoulder, and said, "It's bigger now, Cal. More powerful."

"And you think some of your people are mixed in?"

"Don't know yet, but I'm afraid so."

"Mike Branden is working on some robberies that might tie in with this."

"I know. I'm going to ask for your help again, Cal, when I know more."

Cal fell silent and thought about the difficulties they would face. "This will prove dangerous. Busting it up altogether."

"I don't intend to take on the whole of it, Cal. Just get my own people out. We don't stand a chance of getting back to true Old Order until I accomplish that."

3

Monday, August 7
6:30 P.M.

SHERIFF Robertson was laid out, face down, on one of the metal hospital beds in the emergency room of Joel Pomerene Hospital in Millersburg. His large chest and belly sprawled over the white sheets, and his shoulders bulged over the metal railings on either side. His burned arms hung limply down and his shins hit the metal bar at the foot of the bed. The nurses had stacked two pillows there to soften the edge.

The nurses had also re-hung the IV lines that the paramedics had started, and now a regulator box clicked on a pole next to the bed, as fluids were pumped into Robertson to combat dehydration. They had also strapped his face with a clear blue plastic oxygen mask, and Robertson's head hung over the front edge of the bed, face down.

When he had first arrived, Robertson had insisted on sitting upright on the edge of the bed while they scrubbed the tattered and melted strips of his uniform shirt out of the second- and third-degree burns on his back and on the backs of his arms. He had made a nuisance of himself by taking his oxygen mask off to give orders to the nurses about who'd be coming in to see him and how soon he'd be needed back at the accident scene. Then the first doses of morphine had begun to wear off, and the nurses had convinced him to lie down on his stomach so that the doctors could tend to his burns. One of the doctors had called for another dose of morphine, and the nurses had pushed enough to sedate an average-sized man. Still, he lay awake on his stomach, grumbling about the procedure through his mask. He tried to sit back up, but an ER nurse kept him pinned on his belly. When Lieutenant Dan Wilsher arrived, Robertson was fighting with the nurse to remove his oxygen mask again.

Lieutenant Wilsher pulled a metal chair up to the head of the bed and sat to face the sheriff. He took one of Robertson's hands, partly to help the nurses, and also to let the sheriff know he was there. Wilsher was dressed in street clothes, but his badge was out on his belt, and his face and white shirt were smudged with soot.

Robertson immediately asked, "How's Schrauzer?"

"I'm not sure," Wilsher lied.

Robertson scowled and said, "Get me a report, Dan. I've got to know."

Wilsher answered, "I will, Sheriff, but you've got your own problems to worry about here." He looked back and winced at the scrubbing that was underway on Robertson's back and arms.

A doctor had a scalpel out, cutting skin loose where it was stuck to bits of tattered cloth. One nurse kept a flow of cool saline on Robertson's burns, and another applied ice packs to those areas where the skin was only pink. The darkened skin on Robertson's back had swollen considerably, and near the ugly splotches of third-degree burns, another doctor was cutting shallow lines into the flesh. A third nurse dabbed with a saline swatch at the open wounds to clean them.

Wilsher grimaced and said to Robertson, "We can handle this, Bruce. You're gonna have to stay here for a while."

Robertson groaned and shook his head. "Going back out there tonight. Something's not right."

Wilsher said, "It's OK, Bruce. We're doing everything that

can be done. Even setting up portable floodlights for night work if that's what it takes." Relenting slightly, he reported, "The car is a total loss."

Robertson asked, "Casualties?" His voice sounded muffled through the mask. He tried to lift his head to see Wilsher more directly, but couldn't quite manage the angle.

"A young fellow died in the car," Wilsher said. "He's local. We've got some identification from the license plate, and the family is being asked to come in."

"Won't have a solid ID until Missy Taggert has a look," Robertson said. He shook his head lightly from side to side, remembering the smoke and tremendous heat from the flames.

Wilsher opened a small spiral-bound notebook and said, "There were three others there, besides Schrauzer. Jim Weston in one truck, a Mr. Robert Kent in the second pickup, and Bill MacAfee driving one of his produce trucks. We've got preliminaries from all three."

"Weston owns a surveying company," Robertson said.

"He's surveying those high-end housing developments," Wilsher added.

Robertson grunted. "How about folk in the buggy?"

"Only one, a something 'Weaver.' Taggert pronounced him at the scene. He was turning left into his own driveway when the buggy was hit. The truck driver is dead, too."

"You figure it was the semi?" Robertson asked. He gave out a couple of groans and asked, grousing, "Hey, Doc. You sure you're using morphine?"

The doctor came around to the front of the bed, leaned over, and asked, "You're not comfortable?"

Robertson barked, "No!" and tried to lift his arms to register his dismay.

"We'll push some more," the doctor said and gave the order to the nurse.

Because of his large size and the intense pain, Robertson had worked through the initial doses of morphine quickly. Now the latest dose added its effects, and Robertson began to grow drowsy. Deputy Ricky Niell arrived in a neatly pressed uniform, eyed the sheriff's back, made a pained expression for Wilsher, and took a seat next to the lieutenant. Robertson noticed the uniform and waved his hand feebly to urge Niell closer. Then he let Niell and Wilsher talk, while he struggled to follow the conversation.

"You got second statements from the witnesses?" Wilsher asked Niell.

Niell tapped a finger on his creased uniform breast pocket and said, "Got it all right here," followed by, "How's the sheriff doing?"

Robertson muttered something, but it was muffled by his face mask. Wilsher said, "Fine," obviously not meaning it. He drew close to Niell's ear and whispered, "Nothing yet about Schrauzer. Understand?"

Niell nodded and said, "Sheriff, the skid marks from the semi cab are not that long. And from the hilltop where the professor was, there wouldn't have been more than three, four seconds reaction time, as fast as that truck was going. We figure he hit the buggy at close to forty-five, maybe fifty-five miles an hour, even jackknifed like he was."

Wilsher asked Niell, "The Amishman's name was Weaver?"

"Right. John R. Weaver. I think he's connected up with Melvin Yoder's bunch."

"Weaver would have made that left-hand turn into his drive a thousand times. And it only takes a few seconds to swing one of those ponies off the road, buggy and all."

"So you're wondering why the buggy was standing there long enough to be hit," Niell said.

"That, and why Weaver didn't know a truck was coming."

"There's only about sixty yards from the hilltop down into the low part of the road where Weaver's lane cuts in. That doesn't leave much time for a reaction, even when traffic is slow."

"Then we'll be citing the truck driver for unsafe speed, in any case," Wilsher said.

"Posthumously," Niell said. "Still, you gotta figure the buggy had better odds than just to sit there and get hit like that."

Wilsher thought a while and then asked, "Do we know the point of impact? Some buggy parts were thrown back at least thirty yards."

Robertson tapped his fingers on the metal legs of the hospital bed to get their attention and said, "Cab pushed, kept on." He stalled under the influence of the drugs. "I mean going. After. Twenty yards. Maybe more. Buggy parts at the drive. Parts, Dan."

Wilsher turned to Niell and asked, "Are there any crashed buggy parts right at the turn onto the lane?"

"There are buggy parts everywhere," Niell said, "but the first ones are there, yeah. At the turn onto the lane. The cab came on ahead after the crash and rolled over the point of impact."

Robertson nodded weakly and tapped the legs of the bed insistently. In a faint, muffled voice he asked, "Why jackknifed?"

Wilsher shrugged.

Niell said, "The road curves as it crests there. At high speed, that would have brought the trailer around beside the cab somewhat. Jamming the brakes would have started the jackknife."

Robertson said something like "Umph" and let his head drop. Wilsher made an entry in his notebook.

There was a knock at the door to the small emergency room, and, still dressed in his Amish costume, Professor Branden asked, "All right to come in?"

One of the doctors motioned for Niell and Wilsher to wait in the hall, and then he waved the professor in.

Nodding a silent greeting to the officers as they passed, Branden took one of the two seats at the head of Robertson's bed and asked, "You going to make it all right, Bruce?" He was smiling, but vastly concerned.

He stood up briefly to evaluate the efforts of the doctors and sat back down heavily. Memories of an emergency room long ago surfaced in his mind, from a day in the seventh grade when Robertson had rolled a homemade go-cart on a dirt trail. Branden had been standing on the frame of the go-cart, bracing himself on Robertson's shoulders. He was thrown clear when the go-cart flipped sideways, but Robertson was wedged under the hot lawnmower engine. Branden had fought desperately to lift the heavy engine and wooden frame while Robertson struggled to pull his broken arm out from under the sputtering engine. The burn that day had been bad enough, a patch roughly five inches wide on the back of his arm. The burns today looked like that ugly wound a dozen times over. The seventh-grader had healed quickly. This would be another matter entirely.

Again Branden asked, "Are you all right, Bruce?"

Robertson mumbled, "Drugged," and lightly nodded his head.

Branden looked up to the doctors, and one of them said, "First- and second-degree burns on his back and arms. Several areas of third-degrees, too. We've got most of the shirt cut loose now, and we've had to lance some of the tissue because of the swelling. Mostly, now, we're fighting dehydration and infection, but if I were guessing, I'd say he'll be fine. A smaller man and it'd be a different story, burns as extensive as they are. We figure it's fourteen percent by the body chart system. Now, it mostly depends on how well he cooperates with his recovery regimen."

The professor said, "Oh, brother," and winked at Robertson, well knowing how stubborn the sheriff could be. He leaned over, studied his friend's face, and concluded the sheriff was out with the drugs. Then he said, "Hang in there, Sheriff," and stepped out into the hall to confer with Niell and Wilsher. To them he said, "He got burned up pretty good, once, when we were kids. He'll be fine."

"The nurses say he'll be okay," Ricky said, and added, "They say Bruce was up on the hood of Schrauzer's cruiser, trying to pull him back through the windshield."

"It was a bundle of poles or something," Branden said. "They got Phil out through the driver's door." After reflection, Branden added, "Does Bruce know Phil's dead?"

"No," Wilsher said, "and I'd like to keep it that way for now."

"It looked to me like the eighteen-wheeler knocked the buggy into next week and jackknifed onto the car," the professor said.

Niell said, "That's about it." Turning to the lieutenant, he delivered his report. "We talked again to the three witnesses. They all say the same thing, to a point. The buggy was stopped to make the left turn. The car was stopped behind it, plus Schrauzer in his cruiser, and up came the two other pickups and the produce truck. Then the accounts have it in different orders, but essentially they were all waiting in line when the buggy started its turn, and the back legs of the horse gave out. Two of the witnesses say they also saw Schrauzer backing his cruiser up at that point, and two also report hearing an engine back-fire then."

Branden asked, "How would Phil have known to back up that soon?"

Niell shrugged and Wilsher made a note in his book.

Niell continued. "I think it was the produce truck. That back-fired, I mean. Anyway, they all saw the semi appear at the top of the hill, hit its brakes, trailer started around, the cab smashed into the buggy, and the trailer hit the car sideways and over-turned. The impact threw the car back a ways, and the fire started under it. Probably the gas tank."

Wilsher asked, "What about Weaver?"

"He was crumpled up in what's left of the buggy. About thirty yards back and off to the side in a field."

"Have you laid out most of the buggy?" Wilsher asked. "That'll be important."

"All that we could find so far. We'll use floodlights tonight," Niell said. "What's left, we'll get tomorrow."

Wilsher made another entry in his notebook and asked, "Can either of you figure why Schrauzer was backing his unit up before anybody saw the semi coming over the hill?"

From the end of the hall, Ellie Troyer said, "I've got a better question for you, Dan." Just coming off her shift at the dispatcher's desk in the jail, she was dressed in a black skirt of conservative length and a white blouse. She walked briskly down the hall, hooked an affectionate arm into Niell's, pulled him close, and asked, "How's the sheriff?"

Wilsher said, "He'll be all right. You said there's a better question?"

"Phil called in the wreck himself," Ellie said. "How did he have the time? He said something like 'Big wreck, Ellie. Semi. Buggy. Maybe more.'"

From the emergency room, they heard Robertson pounding on the legs of his hospital bed and saw him waving them into the room.

Ellie led the other three in, and she and Wilsher took the two chairs by Robertson's head.

Robertson's muffled voice came through the plastic mask. "Phil called?" His head was lifted with extreme exertion, and his eyes were high in their sockets, trying to see Ellie's face.

She bent low so she could look into the sheriff's eyes, and Robertson relaxed his neck. Ellie said, "Phil's call was the first one we got on the accident. It was brief, Sheriff, but I got it down that a semi and a buggy were involved. At least that's what I put out on the radio."

Robertson shook his head and mumbled. He reached over and squeezed Dan Wilsher's hand. Softly, they heard him say, "Not enough time," and then he let Wilsher's hand go.

Niell pulled Branden and Wilsher back into the hallway. "He's right," he said. "There wasn't time for Phil to have called it in."

Wilsher frowned and rubbed at his gray hair.

Niell said, "Come out to the parking lot. I've got the poles that smashed through Schrauzer's windshield."

Ellie joined them and they all followed Niell out onto the blacktopped parking lot of the little hospital. Missy Taggert, in a white lab coat, was bent over the open trunk of Niell's cruiser, studying something protruding from the well. She had a tape rule and a blood sample kit, and she was using tweezers to drop a small swatch of hair into a vial.

Taggert's eyes remained fixed on her work in the trunk, but she heard them approaching and said, "Somebody tell me how Bruce is doing before I go nuts out here."

Ellie said, "He's bad off, Missy."

Niell disagreed. "He can handle it."

Branden, sensing great concern in the coroner's voice, encouraged her with, "I think he's going to be fine, Missy."

"Third-degree burns?" she asked, looking up.

"In some places," Branden said gently.

"I'm going in," Taggert announced.

Branden laid his hand softly on her arm and said, "Take a minute and tell us what you've found."

Taggert looked into the trunk and then back to the professor. She eyed the door to the hospital's emergency room and said, "Phil Schrauzer was killed instantly by the blow from this instrument." She reached into the trunk, took hold of the object with both hands, and lifted out a heavy, three-legged surveyor's tripod. The baseplate on top was covered in blood, and clumps of skin, hair, and glass chips were pressed onto it. She stood the tripod on the pavement in front of them. The three wooden legs were painted yellow, and on one of them, lettered in red, was the name J. R. Weaver.

Niell said, "I've stood on that hill. There can't have been more than five seconds between Phil's seeing the semi come over the rise and the time of the impact. Three seconds would be more like it."

Missy said, "All I know is that this tripod came flying out of the back of Weaver's buggy and shot through Schrauzer's windshield before any of the soot from the fires was deposited on the hood of the car."

Ellie asked, "Then how did he manage to call it in?"

Taggert shrugged and said, "I don't know. As far as I can tell, he died too soon to call anyone."

Behind them, they heard a small commotion and when they all turned around they saw Bruce Robertson balancing awkwardly on a single wooden crutch, nurses scrambling to roll his IV stand along behind him, and one doctor storming down the bright hall with a wheelchair.

Robertson balanced on the pavement and glowered at Wilsher. "You didn't tell me he was dead."

Missy Taggert ran up to the big sheriff and steadied him under his free arm. "You're not supposed to be out here, Bruce," she said, and started shouting orders to nurses and doctors alike.

Wilsher took a step or two toward Robertson and said, "The doctors didn't want you to know."

Robertson wavered on his legs and leaned heavily off-balance. Taggert managed to steady him long enough for the professor and Niell to reach him and take hold. The doctor scooted the wheelchair under the sheriff, and Niell and Branden lowered him onto the front edge of it, taking care not to let his back or arms touch the padding of the chair.

From his seat, Robertson looked up to Taggert and said, "I

suppose that means you, Missy. Not wanting me to know about Phil."

Missy nodded and said, "I'm more concerned about you, Sheriff."

Robertson made a dismissive gesture with his hand. The nurses turned him around on the drive, and the doctor pushed a syringe into the port of the sheriff's IV lines.

As they wheeled him back into the hospital, Robertson said, "No time to call. No time to back up," and then he leaned forward and passed out, with two nurses holding him to his seat on the wheelchair.

At the back of Niell's cruiser, Missy said to Branden, "This surveyor's tripod went flying with all the other debris from the buggy. It whipped through the air like everything else out there, and it came through Phil Schrauzer's windshield before he would have had time to blink, much less do anything else. Certainly before he could have made a radio call."

4

THE next morning, Professor Branden stood on the hill where, the day before, he had turned cars back north on 515 and watched through his binoculars as Robertson had struggled to save Phil Schrauzer. Again, he studied the crash scene in the valley below him. There were several cruisers from the State Highway Patrol, and a single line of traffic had been opened on the road. Troopers were posted at each end, with roadblocks to handle the flow of traffic, first in one direction and then in the other.

The semitrailer rig had been righted, and the cab stood on the west side of the road, the charred trailer on the east. A crew of several Amish men worked at the back of the overturned trailer to salvage light oak and dark cherry furniture, transferring it to smaller panel trucks. The blackened hulk of a car sat on its iron wheels where it had burned, and the one-way traffic passed slowly by, drivers rubbernecking at the destruction.

The extent of the fire had been much greater than Branden had realized. The road was blackened with soot for a good thirty yards behind the burnt car, and the grasses, shrubs, weeds, trees, and crops had been burned in large, semicircular patches on either side of the road. The blackened ground ran nearly to John R. Weaver's house, set back forty yards on the west. In the field beyond Weaver's house, the fire had burned to a stand of timber before the firefighters had brought it under control. That stand of timber followed a dried creek bed that edged the western border of the crops and curved around behind Weaver's place, to within twenty yards of the back of his house. On the east, the damage was less extensive, because of the easterly breeze the day before. Here, along the edges of the blackened soil, there were still a few ribbons of smoke lifting gently off the ground.

Once down at the scene, Branden parked on the berm, well back from the investigation, and walked down the slope of the road to the point where Phil Schrauzer's cruiser had backed up and stopped. The professor was dressed in jeans, a green and white Millersburg College T-shirt, and hiking boots. He wore a blue and red Cleveland Indian's ballcap and a pair of mirrored sunglasses.

He saw Schrauzer's cruiser, blackened with soot as far back as the rear doors. On the hood and windshield, under the layer of soot, he could make out the numerous dents and cracks where the car and windshield had been pelted with the debris from the buggy. The windshield was smashed inward over the steering wheel.

The remains of the carriage of the buggy sat off to one side, in the field where it had landed on impact. Several Holmes County deputies were walking slowly over the field, eyes down, gathering the smaller buggy parts to the side of the road. The sheriff's forensics photographer, Eric Shetler, worked slowly there at the berm, taking photos of the debris that had been recovered. As Branden walked in the morning light, the sun was strong from the east, warm on his face and neck, promising another hot and rainless day.

The treads of his boots left waffle patterns in the heated blacktop. The heat reminded him of summer days in Phoenix. Caroline was there now, visiting her mother, a long-standing vacation that had risen to the status of an obligation. Branden had gone with her several times in earlier days, but had been glad, almost relieved, when Caroline had released him from that duty. Now, given the circumstances, he wondered if he shouldn't have gone.

At the site of the impact, a sheriff's deputy had rolled a back-hoe down from its trailer and was working with the bucket to move the dead horse farther away from the pavement. A trooper was measuring the length of skid marks with a rolatape, and another trooper was bending into the cab of the semi, studying the gearshifter.

At the backhoe, Branden called up to the deputy and asked him to settle the horse on its left side. He knelt beside the flank of the horse and examined the crushed and lacerated hip and leg. The right hind leg had been torn viciously loose upon impact with the semi, and now it lay back, in line with the horse's tail, almost completely detached, the severed flesh covered with buzzing flies and gnats. The eviscerated bowels of the horse had poured loose from a gaping tear in the belly.

Next, Branden asked to see the horse laid on its right side, and the deputy on the backhoe started working the scoop under the belly of the horse. After several attempts to roll the horse, the best they could manage was to set the forequarters of the horse on its back, its front legs stiff in the air, with the broken spine of the animal twisted, so that the hindquarters lay reasonably flat. Branden knelt beside the horse again and made a careful inspection along its flank, back toward the hip. The damage here was less severe, but there were deep scratches and skid wounds gouged into the skin so that the horse hair was torn loose in patches, showing pink underneath. The various wounds and road abrasions were laid down as raw, elongated streaks, encrusted with blood.

When Branden stood up from the horse, the deputy on the backhoe shut it down and scrambled off the machine. He walked slowly to Branden and asked, "What are you looking for, Professor?"

Branden held out his hand and said, "I don't believe we've met."

The deputy shook his hand and said, "Stan Armbruster. Newest deputy in the department, which I guess you can tell by the fact that I'm the one out here shoveling dead horse parts off the road."

"Well, Deputy," Branden said, "they say that horse halted in its turn into the lane, and that's what caused the semi to strike the buggy. I was just curious why some of the witnesses would say that it looked like the back legs of the horse seemed to give out, halfway through its turn."

"Find what you were looking for?" Armbruster asked.

"Not at all sure," Branden said. "But I'd be a whole lot happier if we didn't let anybody ship that horse to a fertilizer plant for the time being."

"I'll mention it to the LT," Armbruster said.

"Who's in charge this morning?" Branden asked.

Armbruster scoffed, "The 'flying tires' think they are, but Lieutenant Wilsher's in the house." He made an unfriendly gesture toward the state troopers, and shook his head with the exaggerated disdain typical of rookies.

Branden smiled, thanked Armbruster, reminded him about the horse, walked down the drive to the front porch of John R. Weaver's house, and entered through the screened door. He found himself in a long hallway that led back to a kitchen. The wide floorboards were painted a muted gray. The walls were plain white, and the hallway was trimmed liberally with fine cherry wood.

The kitchen was fitted with a wood stove, a large metal sink with a hand pump for water, and a small wooden table and chair. There were dirty dishes scattered haphazardly about the counters and the sink, and the doorless pantry shelves seemed equally disorganized, stocked with a bounty of dried goods, canned foods, condiments, chips, flour, salt and pepper, herbs, and a couple of dozen two-liter bottles of pop. In one corner, there was a small icebox made of heavy wood, trimmed and bound with ribbons of thick black iron.

Branden glanced through the other doorways off the hall and found a bedroom, a dining room, and a sitting room, all done in the traditional plain Amish fashion of the hallway—gray floors, white walls, and rich cherry trim, the furniture old and unadorned.

Passing back through the kitchen, Branden walked out onto a wide screened porch and found a surprisingly large, boxy addition attached to the back porch, electric lights showing through the windows. An electric line ran to a corner of the addition, and a telephone line came in underneath. There was also a cable TV service wire. The roofline ascended to a peak that was even with the top windows of the second floor of the main house, and, through the tall windows of the new addition, Branden noticed a soaring, vaulted ceiling.

Inside, Branden found Dan Wilsher, in uniform, seated at a modern, black lacquer desk and computer console in the single large room. The console held a monitor, a keyboard, a color printer, and a phone/fax machine. There was also a TV set and a VCR in a far corner, with an easy chair.

The lieutenant was a tall man, somewhat overweight, about fifty years old. He was serious on the job, but handled his duties as lieutenant with a quiet ease that the deputies respected. Out of uniform, he had a reputation as a jokester, and several times he had arranged practical jokes on the sheriff, leaving Robertson to guess who had put the younger deputies up to it. This, too, Branden reflected, had made Wilsher popular with the deputies.

The latest had been one of Wilsher's best, with Phil Schrauzer "walking point." Even with Schrauzer gone, Branden remembered it happily. Phil had backed his car up to the Brandens' garage on a night shift, and he and the professor had off-loaded several boxes containing the sheriff's entire collection of Zane Grey novels, even the first-edition Harper & Brothers. Then they had met all of the other deputies, corporals and captains alike, at the jail, each bringing several old volumes scavenged from garage sales, attics, used book stores, neighbors, grand-parents, even the Internet. The gag had taken the better part of a month to prepare, but the next day, on the shelves where the sheriff's prized Zane Greys normally stood, Robertson found twenty-seven hardbound Nancy Drew mysteries. For as long as he could, he studiously ignored them.

Some days later, when he could contain himself no longer, he started in on the deputies one at a time. It took a week and a half, and it was Schrauzer himself who finally broke. Branden delivered the Zane Greys from his garage to the sheriff, and Robertson cleared out Schrauzer's locker and glued the Nancy Drews together into a tight, immovable pack in the empty space.

Wilsher came out of his reverie, turned to Branden, waved an arm to indicate the whole of the room, and said, "Pretty amazing, don't you think?"

Branden stepped into the room and turned in place to see what Wilsher had indicated. On three of the walls behind him, high up in the vaulted space, there were large game trophies, North American for the most part, but several from Africa, too. There were deer, elk, moose, bear, and a cougar, plus kudu, wildebeest, steenbok, and warthog. As they hung with their eyes looking down into the room, they seemed to press in on Branden like guards in a private art gallery, making the unwanted visi-tor nervous by their unpleasant attentions.

Beneath the trophy heads, along two of the walls, there were wooden shelves, crammed with books, travel guides, and hunt-ing magazines. The room was paneled in dark walnut and finished with a luxuriant blue carpet. In each of the four angled ceiling lines of the vaulted room, there was a large skylight.

Branden stared at the massive heads, feeling vaguely uneasy. Wilsher said, "Come over here and have a seat. It doesn't spook you quite so much when you're sitting down."

Branden crossed the large room and took a seat on a desk chair in front of the monitor. He swiveled gently left and right

and counted the imposing trophy heads, eighteen in all. Then he
pushed up from the chair and walked over to a wall rack beside
the TV, where four hunting rifles were held vertically in place
inside a felt-lined walnut case. The case had slots for five rifles,
but the middle slot was empty. Branden took one of the rifles
down and sighted the scope through a window onto a distant
hillside. He opened the bolt and inspected the chamber. Next he
studied the scope, a Leupold variable-power model, with extra-
ordinarily fine, custom cross hairs. The rifle itself was a classic
Remington 700 series, mounted to a modern, black composite
stock. Branden took a bill out of his wallet, wrapped it around
the barrel, and slid it freely between the barrel and the stock.
To Wilsher he commented, "Free-floated barrel," with admira-
tion, and stood the rifle back in the case where he had found it.

Wilsher said, "Guess he was a big hunter," and continued
browsing through the desk drawers.

Branden came over to the desk, and said, "Those aren't run-
of-the-mill firearms."

Wilsher turned in his chair to face Branden and asked, "So
how do you figure a guy in a buggy makes it over to Africa to
hunt dangerous game?"

Branden shrugged and said, "Better yet, figure a guy in a
buggy with a modern, electric addition off his back porch."

The two fell silent for a moment and then Wilsher turned
back to the desk. Branden rose to study the contents of a tall
metal filing cabinet next to the computer console. He opened
the top drawer labeled "Lands Owned." The other drawers
were marked "Lands Sold," "Lands Leased," and "Prospects."

Wilsher said, "Weaver has land deals dating back to 1986,
as far as I can make out."

Branden studied the numerous file folders in the "Lands
Owned" drawer and said, "He also owned half of several townships. Come look at this, Dan."

Wilsher stood up and went over to the filing cabinet. Branden had one file opened, the pages laid flat on top of the drawer. There was a bill of sale, a record of the auction price, a receipt for cash, copies of the deed, and a computer version of a surveyor's drawing attached to the deed. The drawing bore the initials JRW and was dated "Mar 06 '96." A separate page described the parcel in detail, giving its location in township, parcel, and lot numbers, along with a reference to county and township roads. In pencil, there was listed an estimated value on the land. The price had been erased several times and updated values had been penciled in over the old ones. In the lower right-hand corner was a notation reading "B. Sommers, 8%." Branden put the folder away and began counting the folders in the drawer. When he was finished, he said, "Thirty-nine properties, scattered over three townships."

Wilsher whistled and said, "Big game hunter and land baron, too." He watched curiously as Branden opened the drawer marked "Lands Sold."

In this drawer, nearly fifty manila folders were packed together so tightly that it would have been difficult to add another to the collection. Branden worked a few of the folders loose and laid one open on top of the drawer. It contained the same types of documents as the folders in the first drawer, but on the outside of each of these folders there was a tabulation of dates, purchase price, sale price, and profit. Several had notations in the lower right corners about B. Sommers, 8 percent here, 7 or 10 percent elsewhere. Wilsher began pulling folders, and Branden ran a tally in his head. When they had worked through the drawer, Branden stood silently for a long moment, and then closed the drawer slowly, saying, "That's 2.3 million in profit, in the last five years alone."

Wilsher chuckled and ran his fingers through his hair. "Big game hunter, land baron, and millionaire," he ventured. After a moment's hesitation, he added, "No wonder the good farm land in this county has been disappearing!"

Branden nodded. He drummed his fingers on top of the filing cabinet, looking disconcerted. He glanced around the room again and settled his gaze on John Weaver's black lacquer desk with its computer. He said, "Did you find anything in there to suggest where he's got all that money stashed in a bank, or are we going to find it buried in cans out in the backyard?"

Wilsher sat at the desk, opened the top right-hand drawer, and pulled out a folded, leather-bound collection of papers. He dropped the package on the desk and said, "He's got a trust fund at the bank in Millersburg. The same B. Sommers on these folders is listed as trustee."

"Britta Sommers," Branden said. "I went to school with her. She was popular. Junior prom queen the year I graduated. Jimmy Weston was her escort. I've known her all my life."

"The Jim Weston who was out here yesterday?" Wilsher asked.

"Yes," Branden said. "He was a sophomore. A little scat-back runner on the football team. Ran with the 'in crowd.' Britta was something else in those days."

"Still is, from what I hear," Wilsher said, leading.

"Like I said, junior prom queen and then senior court the next year. She was my eighth-grade sweetheart, but she threw me over for a football player. Little Jimmy Weston. If I remember right, she and Weston stayed together even after she left for college. They never married, though. She found someone better after college. At least she thought he was better."

Wilsher sat and thought for a moment, studying the trust papers. Then he said, "I guess Sommers has got some work to do, then. Now that Weaver's dead, I mean."

"You going to call her out here?" Branden asked. He took the leather trust folder from Wilsher and leafed idly through the pages.

Wilsher took the folder back, folded the leather pouch,

snapped it shut, and said, "I'll start by running these into Millersburg."

"Let me do that," Branden said, and held out his hand for the folded leather pouch. "I know Britta Sommers well, Dan. I'm going back to town for an afternoon conference, but I can get the papers to her first thing in the morning."

Wilsher smiled mischievously and asked, "What are you long-hairs doing today? Debating who really won the Civil War?" There was a wide grin on his face as he dropped the trust papers into Branden's hand.

"Actually," Branden said, amused, using a professorial tone, "if you take the long-term view, you might argue that the eventual loss of the big manufacturing industries in the North and the resurgence of Southern life that we're seeing today . . ."

Wilsher cut him off with a wave of the hand and quipped, "Oh, brother. Why'd I even ask?"

When the two had walked back through the house to the front, they found Deputy Armbruster arguing with a man in a baggy suit. The squat little man complained, "I'm supposed to be the first one to go over the scene," as Wilsher and Branden walked up.

Wilsher asked, "We got a problem here, Stan?"

The man in the suit turned to Wilsher, took in the lieutenant's gold bars, and said rancorously, "I'm Robert Cravely. Insurance. And you've moved all of the buggy parts, Lieutenant."

Wilsher responded calmly, "We've merely laid them out beside the road to clear a lane for traffic."

Cravely removed a wallet badge from his inside suit pocket, displayed it briefly, and said pompously, "I am a specialist in buggy crashes. I've been retained by the insurance carrier for the furniture company that owns that truck over there. I study debris scatter. Impact analysis. And you should not have moved anything until I had a chance to go over the scene."

Branden touched Wilsher's arm, and, holding back a laugh, said, "I'm gonna take these papers to Sommers in the morning."

Wilsher nodded and turned back to the insurance agent. As Branden walked away, he could hear the lieutenant explaining, somewhat indignantly, why he thought it more important to clear a lane for traffic than to have expert analysis of buggy debris, considering that they had three solid witnesses who had observed the crash firsthand.

At his truck, Branden tossed the leather pouch onto the passenger's seat, climbed in behind the wheel, hit the ignition, and swung around on the pavement. As he climbed back up to Walnut Creek, he used his cell phone to call Melissa Taggert in her coroner's labs. He told her what he had discovered about the horse, asked her to have a look herself, and then explained why, and what he thought she would find in her inspection.

5

CAL Troyer walked among the pews of his little church house, laying down one-page outlines for Wednesday night's Bible study. He finished and sat down in the last pew, remembering earlier days when he had known Andy Weaver as a single Amishman from the Melvin P.'s, a prosperous district mostly to the north of Walnut Creek, in the Goose Bottoms and the hills beyond. Although many things had happened to precipitate a crisis in the district, the central problem had been, in Andy Weaver's opinion, that Yoder was an increasingly liberal bishop, and Weaver hadn't liked it then at all. As the new bishop, he surely didn't like it any better now.

But such had always been Andy Weaver's convictions—that a conventional, Old Order lifestyle was the best possible life for a family. Living close to the land. Far from a city's temptations.

And so there had been a falling out when Bishop Yoder's rulings had grown too liberal for Weaver. Lights. Electric tools. Printers and computers. Fax machines. All in the businesses at first, but inexorably moving into the homes as well. And when Andy R. Weaver had had his fill, he broke away and moved his family to a more conservative district in Pennsylvania.

Funny, Cal thought, how different the older brother had turned out. John R. Weaver had taken to modern things as if he were born to the electronic age. Land had been his obsession, and land aplenty he had. For him, it hadn't been enough to tend a single farm. Or to raise a family. His business dealings had become a wife to him, and his land holdings were like his children. But that was all gone, now, with J.R.'s untimely death.

Two brothers, then. One enticed by Melvin P. Yoder's flirtation with the modern world. The other repelled by it. Now, Andy R. Weaver was going to try to straighten out the whole sorry mess in his district north of Walnut Creek.

Cal pushed up from the wooden pew and gave a final look around the sanctuary. Everything was ready for Wednesday services. The lesson would teach itself from his outline. He walked out, locked up, and pulled the doors open on his truck, to let the heat out.

While he waited there, a plain black buggy pulled into the gravel parking lot, and Andy Weaver got out and tethered his horse to a light pole in the corner of the lot. He came slowly over to Troyer, lifted his hat off, and wiped his brow on his shirt sleeve. Cal closed up his truck and motioned Weaver into the little story-and-a-half brick parsonage beside the church. In the kitchen, cooler with the shades drawn, the two sat at a little formica table and shared a half pitcher of iced tea that Cal had made the day before. Cal waited for Weaver to make some mention of his troubles.

Andy fished out a wedge of lemon and bit into it, puckering as he chewed. "Lost a family this morning," he confided after a pause.

Cal drained his tea, poured more for himself and Weaver, and waited.

"I had three of the men together to rule on electric lights, and one balked. I told him he could find a liberal group up east of Trail."

Cal whistled.

"Make an example of one, you see," Andy observed.

"You think the rest will hold tight?"

"I believe so. I had plenty of nominations from the people, and they all saw me draw the lot to become Bishop."

"It's almost asking too much, Andy," Cal said without guile. "You're taking them backwards, and most of them are sticking with you."

"You'd have expected otherwise?"

Cal nodded quietly.

"You're right," Weaver sighed.

"If you can keep 80 percent, that will be good."

"This morning I am only two for three," Weaver said, distantly.

"There's still the two men who stayed with you," Cal encouraged.

Weaver managed to produce a wry smile. "They came into town with me this afternoon. Down at the light company, telling them to take out the electric wires."

"A victory, then," Cal said.

"For now."

"You knew you'd lose a few, Andy."

Andy paused and changed the subject with a distasteful look on his face. Heavily, he said, "I've made no progress identifying our cultists, but some families seem afraid of their teenagers."

Cal's forehead wrinkled as his eyebrows lifted questioningly. To lighten the mood, he asked, "You remember Mony Hershberger's Ben?"

A brief smile broke out on Weaver's face, and he laughed softly. "Mailboxes."

"I'll bet he busted up twenty before they caught him," Cal added.

Grinning, Weaver said, "Mony's Ben was always a little 'touched in the head,' Cal."

"Just a little?"

"You remember that barn fire his father had?"

"That was Ben?" Cal asked, surprised.

"He didn't mean it. Just trying to light a pipe, was all," Weaver said. He smiled, looked out the kitchen window for a spell, and then appeared to slump in his chair. "You know my older brother died Monday in a crash in front of his house?"

"J.R. Yes. I'm sorry," Cal said.

"I wish I could say the same," Andy blurted. "I didn't mean that," he added instantly. His frown was heavy, and he shook his head slowly back and forth.

Cal sat motionless.

Weaver peered directly into Troyer's eyes and said, "It looks like my brother swindled eight of my men, Cal."

Cal appeared skeptical.

"Truly," Weaver asserted. "Eight men got letters yesterday canceling the notes on their farms."

"That's not possible," Cal said.

"I'd have agreed with you. But there's something about some 'Lease to Own' contracts, and I've got to sort through to the bottom of it all in less than a week."

Cal leaned back a ways in his chair, clasped his fingers behind his head, and blew out air, saying, "Whew!"

"It gets worse," Weaver said nervously.

Cal waited, still leaning back.

"Two families have got at least one son each they won't talk about. There's gossip. I told one father I intended talking to his son, and he grew nervous. Told me in so many words that that might not be prudent! Of course their wives wouldn't say anything at all."

"What kind of secret can anyone keep among the Amish?" Cal asked, intending no disrespect.

Weaver said, "They all know about it, all right. Just no one's talking."

"You're right," Cal said, bringing his arms down to the table. "That beats electric problems any day."

"I think Melvin Yoder must have gone far more liberal than I realized."

Cal shook his head.

"It's not everyone," Weaver explained.

"Still," Cal said.

"Have you got a lot going this summer, Cal?"

"Just the usual."

"You think you and Mike Branden could help on the land matter?"

"Not with the boys?"

"That will be my little problem for a while."

"You want me to talk to Mike first, or get going on it myself?"

"I need you and Branden to come out and talk with the men."

"Your place?"

"Yoder's old house. Temporarily."

"You said they all got a letter?"

Weaver nodded.

"We'll need to see that," Cal said.

Weaver nodded and frowned heavily. "Can you get out to the house Friday morning?"

"I'll have to check."

"You sure you've got the time, Cal?"

Cal said, "Of course—just like the old times," and waited.

Weaver sat with an unhappy expression and eventually said, "The way those letters read, my brother sold the land out from under eight of my families just before he died."

6

AFTER a light breakfast, Branden took the leather pouch containing J. R. Weaver's trust papers off the kitchen table and stepped into the stuffy garage. He put the garage door up, and bright light flooded in on an assaulting wave of dry heat. He rolled down the windows on his truck, backed out onto the cul-de-sac where his brick colonial stood near the campus, and drove down into town with the truck windows open, the temperature already showing ninety-two degrees on the bank display just south of the courthouse square. He waited for traffic to clear on Clay Street and swung into the bank lot, his tires crackling on the heat blisters in the blacktop. As he walked toward the two-story brick bank building, pavement heat lifting through the soles of his worn sandals, he held J. R. Weaver's leather pouch under his left arm, and flipped through his wallet for the photocopy he had made yesterday from his senior yearbook—Brittany Sommers in her high school cheerleader's uniform, captain of the squad. Britta was the smallest of the lot, the confident, scrappy little girl smiling at the camera from the top position of a human pyramid, her black hair shiny and long, the fall sweater-and-skirt uniform revealing, in the young girl, the beautiful form she would carry as a woman. He shook his head, remembering her fondly, and slid the photo back into his wallet, intending to tease her about it if he got the chance.

In the shade under the portico of the bank's main doors, Branden used a handkerchief to dry sweat beads on his hands and arms, the back of his neck, and face. He was dressed in blue jeans and a plain yellow T-shirt. He had made the appointment yesterday, and he had stopped at Chester's shop for a haircut and a trim. Now he used the bank window as a mirror to comb hair and beard into place. He studied his reflection in the window glass and smiled at himself, realizing that he hadn't needed the haircut. He took out his handkerchief again, this time to dry the leather pouch he was carrying.

He lingered in the shade of the portico while a line of customers spilled out of the bank, and he noticed the brief rush of cool air through the open door. An unkempt man came out through the main doors, stopped short at sight of the professor, and stood blocking the doorway, eyeing Branden up and down with a spiteful expression, until he was forced to move aside by people wanting to get through the door. He moved closer to Branden and blurted, "Look, Branden. My ex talks about you all the time."

"Arden Dobrowski," Branden said contemptuously. "You're not allowed within five hundred yards of Britta Sommers."

"That lying tramp is trying to freeze me out of . . . "

He would, apparently, have said considerably more, but Branden took him forcibly under the arm, spun him against the outside brick wall of the bank, jabbed two stiff fingers into Dobrowski's chest and barked, "You'll not speak about Britta that way."

Dobrowski tried to force Branden's arm away as he squirmed against the hot bricks.

Branden stiffened his arm and took hold of Dobrowski's shirt. Coldly, he said, "If I hear you talking like that about Britta

Sommers, I'm going to land on you like a pile driver, Arden. You understand? I've done it before, and under the circumstances, I'll do it again."

Dobrowski took Branden's fist, pulled it away from his chest, and stepped sideways. "She's my ex, thanks to you, and I'll talk about her any way I please."

Branden said, "You've been warned," and felt pressure in his temples as he remembered why he would never tolerate such comments from Dobrowski. He took a combative step forward and glared with animosity at Dobrowski in the bright light on the bank's front lawn, his eyes ablaze with the heat of ugly memories and utter disgust. Dobrowski stomped angrily out into the parking lot, rubbing at his shoulder.

Back in the shade, Branden watched Dobrowski get into a small, rusty car. Dobrowski labored at cranking down the windows on both sides of his car, and started the sputtering engine. When he swung around past the front of the bank, he scowled at Branden and made a vulgar gesture. Then he stopped, checked his rearview mirror, backed into the lot again, took a spot facing the entrance where Branden stood, shut off the engine, and stared at Branden spitefully. Branden laughed, shook his head, and stepped into the cold air of the bank.

Inside, he asked one of the managers to let him into the men's room in a corner out of view, and there he dried his face and neck again, straightened his shirt, touched up his hair and beard, came out, and took the steps to the second floor, where the trust division had its offices along both sides of a long, carpeted hall. At the door to each office, a secretary worked at a desk in the wide hall.

Britta Sommers's secretary used her phone to announce the professor and admitted Branden directly. Branden walked into a well-ordered, modern office done in mahogany, black lacquer, and red leather, and found Brittany Sommers crossing the carpet to him, arms outstretched. She was still petite, with short black hair that seemed silky and looked shiny. Her gray business suit hid nothing of the youthful beauty Branden remembered from high school. She came up to him eagerly, reached her arms behind his neck, and pulled him to her aggressively. She kissed him impetuously on the mouth before he could turn away, and with her head tilted back, she said, "Mike. Mike. Mike. Why didn't I marry you?"

He dropped the leather pouch onto a table beside a floor lamp and chair, reached behind his head with both hands, pulled her hands down, maneuvered them in front of his chest, and took a deep breath as he pushed her back. "Britta," he said gently, "eighth-grade romances are such sweet affairs. Who would ruin those memories with a marriage?"

She held his blue eyes with her green, smiled dreamily, and sighed, "She calls you Michael, doesn't she?"

"Caroline?"

"Who else?" she said and pushed closer. "I'm going to call you Michael, too."

"You're still a flirt, Britta," he chided, and stepped free of her grasp. "As I recall, you threw me over for a football player."

"The captain, Michael," Britta said in a petulant tone. "Not just a player." Her eyes sparkled mischief, and she whispered, "I'll just call you Michael when we're alone." She stepped back and ran her gaze over his medium frame, assessing the muscles under his T-shirt. Up close again, she ran her fingers through his hair at the temples and said, "More gray than I remember, Michael."

The professor blushed and said, "If eighth-grade love affairs ever truly lasted, you'd be the one, Britta. You'd be the one."

With a triumphant smile, she spun around and swayed back to her desk. Once on the other side of the desk, however, she seemed to stiffen and lose some of her sparkle. She motioned for Branden to take a seat in a red leather chair, pointed at the leather pouch on the table by the lamp, and said, "What do you have there?"

Branden retrieved the pouch, eased himself into the plush chair, and said, "John R. Weaver's trust."

"Oh," Britta said, pensive. She sat behind her desk and said, "Somebody's been working overtime down at the sheriff's."

"They want me to ask you about the trust. We got the papers out at his house, and there are a lot of other papers out there that indicate you and Weaver had a land deal or two going on. They'll want to know about that, too."

"That's awfully nosy," Britta scolded, "sending you over here like that."

"You're Weaver's trust officer, Britta, and his death might not have been an accident."

Sommers's eyebrows arched, and she asked, "Not an accident?"

"We don't know yet."

"I suppose you're working for the sheriff again."

"For the sheriff's office. The sheriff himself was injured at the accident scene."

"Bull in a china shop, if you ask me."

"It's a delicate matter, Britta. It's only me. And for now, I just want a sketch of what Weaver's trust will do, now that he's dead. And some background on his land dealings."

"His latest deal was the big one," Britta said. "I've got a little piece of the action. It's my 'walk-away' money, Michael. The land sales, that is. I'm selling out everything I've got invested in this county to a developer in Cleveland and moving to Nashville."

"Selling out everything?"

"Land, house, job, and furniture. It all goes. I'm moving south to live with my son. Take care of him."

"How is he?"

"He's autistic."

"I know that, Britta."

"He's been living in an institution near Vanderbilt, in Nashville, since I divorced Arden. Now I think it's time to put a stop to that. I'm selling off everything and moving down there to be with him. To take care of him myself."

"Will you have enough?" Branden asked.

Sommers laughed spiritedly. "Since you, Michael, all the men in my life have been losers. Not me. I invested all of Arden's alimony payments in the stock market in the nineties. I learned about land deals from watching John Weaver work. And I started a little company with him. Sommer Homes. Kinda catchy, don't you think? It's only a portion of what Weaver had going throughout the county, but the profits have been marvelous."

"I've seen some of the documents on Weaver's land deals," Branden said. "He was good at it, if his ledgers tell the truth."

"The best," Britta said. "That's why I threw in with him. I showed him how to invest money, and he showed me how to make it."

"With Sommer Homes?"

"That was the core of it, but I need to have a little privacy, Michael." She winked at him.

"So it's the Sommer Homes holdings, plus some?" Branden asked.

"More than just the land, Michael," she said. "Like I said, I'm getting out quick and moving south. All of the deals haven't closed, but with Weaver dead, I collect another half-million, with partner's insurance."

Branden leveled his gaze at her pensively, aware that she was toying with him.

"Oh, come now, Michael," Britta said. "You wouldn't expect a woman to go unprotected. I work partner's insurance into all of my companies. Gonna make out pretty well on this one."

"All of the deals haven't closed?"

Britta smiled and said, "We signed a binding agreement on the land sales to Holmes Estates last week."

"When?" Branden asked.

"Friday. Why?"

"I'm just trying to figure why anyone would want Weaver dead."

"Weaver was finished with his part of the deals," Britta said. "There are still a few things for me to finish up this week, and then I'll be headed south." She smiled mischievously and added, "Come with me, Michael."

Branden grinned and scolded her with a wagging finger.

Britta smiled and said, "Can't blame a girl for trying." Then she added, seriously, "I'm selling it all, Michael. For Danny. Stocks, land holdings, everything. I've transferred all the proceeds into a trust that I began for Danny three years ago—a portfolio that provides a trust fund for him and a good life for me. I've given my notice and handed over my accounts to other trust officers. By this time next week, my house will be on the market, and I'll be in Nashville, making arrangements for a new life for my son. New doctors, better schools, everything. I'm getting out, Michael, and I'm getting out on top."

Branden smiled, openly happy for her. "You've done well, Britta." More seriously, he added, "What about Arden Dobrowski?"

"He's out," Britta said, instantly cold.

Branden questioned with his eyes.

"Arden's a loser, Michael. Like I told you, they all were. All the men in my life except you. I never should have dropped you for Weston. You know better than anyone why I divorced Arden. Anyway, he paid alimony until about a year ago, when his car lots went belly up, and he filed for bankruptcy. Now he's in the courts, trying to worm his way into our son's trust. Wants to handle the money jointly. It's not enough that he begs spending money off me. I'm tired of it. I just told him that I'm leaving."

"Bumped into him outside," Branden said. "Had to rough him up a bit, the way he was talking."

"About me, I suppose."

Branden shrugged. "So he doesn't like it that you're moving?"

"Poor baby," Britta quipped.

"Has he ever tried to hurt you again?"

"He knows not to try. I've learned how to hit back."

Branden shook his head, respecting her boldness. He thought of the leather pouch and asked, "How about the trust fund for Weaver?"

Sommers stood up with her hand stretched out for the papers. "Those are private papers, Michael," she said officiously. "Confidential. The sheriff has got no right to be looking into that."

"If Weaver's death was truly an accident," Branden said, "you're altogether right."

"It was an accident," Britta claimed.

"I'm not so sure."

"Until you are sure," Britta said, "I'll have to insist that you give those documents to me."

Branden hesitated, studied Britta's expression, smiled, relented, and handed her the documents.

"I've got a feeling, Britta, that you'll soon be handing those papers back," he said.

"Show me conclusively that he was murdered, and I will, Michael."

She dropped the pouch into a side drawer and came around to the front of her desk. She took the professor's hands, lifted him up from the leather chair, and slipped an arm around his waist. With a little nudge, she escorted him to the door, stopped him there, gazed into his eyes, opened the door for him and said, "Come see me at the house, once, before I leave."

In the stairwell to the lobby, Branden wiped the lipstick from his lips and put the handkerchief back in his pocket. He pushed through the door to the lobby and looked around, embarrassed to think that someone might have seen him.

The morning's heat assaulted him again at the bank's doors. Outside, a brave little sprinkler fanned back and forth over a stricken patch of grass in the fierce sun. He cupped a palm over his eyes and scanned the parking lot for his truck. Arden Dobrowski stepped out of his small sedan and marched across the blacktop toward Branden. Branden scowled and headed for his truck. Dobrowski caught him halfway and took hold of the professor's arm.

Branden wrenched his arm free, glowered at him aggressively, and barked, "What do you want, Dobrowski?"

"What'd that cheating scum say . . . ?"

Midsentence, Branden shifted his weight to square up to Dobrowski. He balanced a left fist in front of his chest, feet planted wide, smashed his right fist into Dobrowski's face, and stepped slowly to his truck, leaving Dobrowski on the blacktop, bent over and bleeding profusely from the nose.

7

BRANDEN entered Millersburg's boxy red brick jail through the main door opposite the Civil War monument on the courthouse lawn. He found Ellie Troyer taking a call behind the wooden counter where the old radio dispatcher's equipment was stacked beside her gray metal desk. Branden let himself through the swinging door at the left end of the counter and poured a cup of coffee, using one of the white Styrofoam cups stacked beside the pot. He glanced left, down the pine-paneled hallway of the jail's offices, came back through the swinging door, and leaned sideways against the counter, sipping coffee while Ellie finished her phone call. She hung up, spoke briefly in the ten-codes at the radio's microphone, and swiveled her chair to the professor. She frowned and said, "The sheriff's not much better at all."

Branden sipped his coffee, smiled encouragement, and said, "He'll be all right, Ellie," for pretense.

Ellie said, "Humph," and added, "Ricky and I tried to see him this morning, but they wouldn't let us in."

Less confident, Branden shrugged. "They're just being cautious with his burns."

"The sheriff's not as tough as you think he is," Ellie said, scolding.

"He'll pull through," Branden said, uneasy that Ellie Troyer, usually so solid and upbeat, seemed downhearted. "Do you know something I don't know?" Branden asked, an anxious concern for the sheriff creeping out from a vulnerable place in his heart where he could not contemplate the truth.

"There's a look in Missy Taggert's eyes," Ellie said. "She's been assisting in his treatments, and she's worried."

"It's probably more like the doctors over there are taking orders from Missy," Branden said and smiled weakly. "She likes him, you know."

Ellie nodded, and her eyes acquired a distant look.

"Something else?" Branden asked.

Ellie stood, brushed the creases out of her long skirt and adjusted the pin that held her hair back. Sighing, she glanced around her work area as if she were looking for something to do. Then she took a deep breath and said, "Oh I don't know. It could be anything. It's not right around here with Bruce gone. Kessler is on vacation in Wyoming, and Captain Newell has taken over the sheriff's office. I don't know. Maybe I worry more than I should."

"Bruce is tough enough to pull through, Ellie."

"I'm more worried about you and Cal Troyer, if it proves he isn't."

"We've all been friends for a long time."

"Cal's got Bruce on a prayer chain. Round the clock prayers. His whole church is at it."

"You'd expect anything else?" Branden asked softly, not letting on that the news had startled him.

A mist appeared over Ellie's eyes, and she turned her head.

Branden smiled sympathetically and asked, "Is Newell in the sheriff's office now?"

Ellie turned back around with a handkerchief held loosely in her fingers.

Branden said, "I think you miss the sheriff, Ellie."

"No!" Ellie said with obvious sarcasm, and dried her eyes.

"Ellie, if Missy Taggert is directing Bruce's treatments, then he couldn't be in better hands. She'll get him what he needs, whatever it takes, and she'll take him somewhere else, if she can't get it here. She's a strong and determined woman. She cares for him. And he's going to pull through." He had spoken it as a promise to himself, perhaps also as a prayer.

Ellie nodded and smiled weakly.

Branden let a calming moment pass and then asked, "Is the captain taking visitors?"

The radio came alive, and Ellie nodded yes, waving Branden down the hall as she sat down and rolled up to the console. Branden passed through the swinging door, tossed his coffee cup into a wastebasket beside Ellie's desk, and heard her taking details from a deputy at the scene of an accident.

At the sheriff's office, Branden rapped his knuckles on the door, entered, and found Captain Robert "Bobby" Newell staring blankly at papers on the sheriff's big cherry desk. Newell glanced up, motioned Branden to a seat, and said, "I can't believe the sheriff does all this paperwork."

Newell had the powerful build of a weightlifter, and he filled out his uniform dramatically. With his short brown hair, square jaw, and heavy eyebrows he appeared rugged, capable. His large arms bulked at his sides, straining the fabric of his black and gold uniform shirt, and his powerful hands seemed out of place handling mere paper.

Branden took a seat in front of the desk and said, "Bobby, I'm sure he lets Ellie do most of that."

Newell pushed his chair back from the desk and looked puzzled. Branden said, "I think she could use something to do out there."

Newell said, "That sounds more like it." He pulled forward, began stacking the papers together, and said, "Couldn't figure how Robertson did all of it himself."

"You hear anything about how he's doing?" Branden asked.

"Stable, but not too much better is what the doctors say."

"And your investigation into Weaver?"

"Dan Wilsher's been going through some of Weaver's papers."

"I was out there with him yesterday," Branden said.

"He told me that," Newell said. "Also said you were going to talk to Brittany Sommers about the Weaver trust."

"Did that this morning, Bobby. He and Sommers had just finished a big land deal with an outfit up in Cleveland."

"Ordinary stuff?" Newell asked.

"Seems to be," Branden said, and added, "The accident still troubles me."

"Why?"

"That horse shouldn't have gone down that way."

"Taggert said you had her looking into something."

"An autopsy," Branden said.

"On the horse?"

"I think there's something there."

"Why?"

Branden shrugged. "A hunch. People report hearing a backfire, and that horse dropped over funny."

Newell rubbed his thick fingers on his chin, thinking.

"You've still got some men on the case?" Branden asked.

Newell nodded yes. "Wilsher's going through Weaver's office with Niell, and he's got two more deputies gathering facts about the accident. Then we'll turn it all over to the highway patrol. It's their case, anyways."

"Give it more time, Bobby," Branden offered. "I don't think it was an accident."

"You got that when you spoke with Sommers?"

"No."

"Do you have something from Weaver's trust papers that Dan Wilsher needs to know about?"

"No, but . . . "

"Is there anything you can cite, other than your hunch about the horse?"

"No, Bobby. I just think there are loose ends, and I'd like to see us staying on it a while longer."

"OK, but my deputies are stretched pretty thin, Mike."

"I can work it as hard as I want," Branden said.

"Doing what?"

"The personal stuff. You know, Bobby. Things the highway patrol isn't going to get into. More from the witnesses, maybe."

"We've got complete statements from MacAfee, Kent, and Weston," Newell said. "Niell interviewed each of them twice, at the scene."

"Memories change, Bobby. There's the insurance angle and the land dealings. I can stay on it as long as I want, and it won't cost your deputies a minute. I'll just work the edges. Witnesses again. Land deal angles. Trust funds. You know. Anywhere, really. Besides, there's Taggert's horse autopsy that hasn't come in yet."

"Those buggy robberies are still a concern to me, Mike. Those masks make me nervous."

"We knew there'd be trouble from that crowd someday," Branden said. "My concern is that word about me is going to get out."

"You think anyone knows?"

"Just two families. One where I borrow the rig, and one where I water the horse."

"There should have been gossip by now."

"Hasn't seemed to be, yet," Branden said.

"You've probably got only a few more rides before those kids find out."

"I might need only one or two more, Bobby."

Newell drummed his fingers on the desk and said, "Ricky Niell thinks he knows a way to track 'em down."

"The sooner the better," Branden offered.

Newell said, "OK," and came around from behind the desk. He gathered up the papers and said, "Let's go see Ellie."

Out at her dispatcher's station, Newell asked, "Ellie, is this the kind of stuff you do for Robertson?"

Ellie took the stack of papers and forms from the captain, fanned through the top ones, and said, "These should have been done already."

Newell said, "Can you do them?"

"You don't think Bruce does them himself?" Ellie said, laughing.

"Well, then. I've got my own sack of rocks to carry," Newell said, and disappeared into the locker room at the far end of the hall.

Ellie waited until he had gone and said, "I suppose I've got you to thank for this, Professor."

Branden smiled mischievously. "I thought you could use the distraction."

"Thanks a heap, Doc," Ellie said and started whistling softly as she sorted the forms and papers.

8

WHEN the doorbell rang at the Brandens' house, the professor was lying motionless on a long couch in the living room, with the lights turned off and curtains drawn. For nearly an hour, he had been thinking about J. R. Weaver's death and Britta Sommers's financial triumph. He rose slowly on stiff legs and opened the front door. In the bright light, he saw a man and a woman in upper middle age, holding hands. They were both dressed haphazardly, as if the cares of recent days had not permitted them the luxury of careful grooming. The woman had evidently applied some makeup, but her mascara was running.

"I'm Denny Smith," the man said, "and this is my wife Lenora. May we speak with you, Professor?"

As Branden hesitated slightly, the woman's eyelids fluttered, and a sheen of new tears appeared. She held a tissue beneath her eye and dabbed mascara from her cheek. "It was our son Brad who died in the fire out on 515," she whispered.

Branden held the screen door open, and motioned them inside without comment. When he had closed the door against the outside heat, he ushered them into the darkened living room and turned on a small lamp on a table next to two swivel-rocker Lazy Boys opposite the couch.

"I've been keeping it cool," he said, "but we can turn on more lights if you prefer."

"Not on my account," Mrs. Smith said, and sat in one of the chairs next to her husband.

Branden asked, "Can I fix you something cold to drink?"

They both declined, so he sat down on the edge of the couch and said, "How can I help you?"

"We want to hire you," Mr. Smith said.

"Why, Mr. Smith? Because of your son?"

"Please, it's Denny. And yes, to investigate our son's death."

"I'm already doing that, Denny. In a somewhat official capacity."

"We want more," Mrs. Smith said forcefully. "That truck driver was drunk." Anger seemed to replace her tears, and she sat up straight on the edge of the rocker and eyed Branden with determination.

"I can tell you what we learn, as the investigation proceeds," Branden said.

Denny Smith said, "Please, Professor. We can get that ourselves from the sheriff's office. We want someone to go to Chicago. Track down this trucking company. Find out what you can about that driver."

"It sounds like you're building a case," Branden said.

"We want to do what we can for our son," Lenora said.

"Things are very preliminary right now," Branden offered.

"I want to put them out of business," Denny insisted. "Lenora and I. We're not going to bury our son and just let it go at that."

"I'm sorry, but I can't go to Chicago right now," Branden said.

"What do we have to do, Professor?" Denny complained, sitting back and shaking his head.

Lenora took hold of her husband's hand and said, "It's all right, Denny. We'll do it ourselves. We always have, anyway." She looked reproachfully at Branden.

"You can do better than me, at any rate," Branden said. "I don't know Chicago. And I'm not a licensed investigator."

Lenora had her purse open now, and she stuffed her tissues into the bottom of it. There was a look of determination in her eyes, almost bordering on spite. "If you won't help us, we'll do it ourselves."

"Mrs. Smith," Branden said. "Please. I really can't help you. But you don't have to do it yourselves, either."

Lenora was on her feet, now, and she had her husband standing, too.

Branden stood up and said, "Hire a Chicago detective."

Lenora stood in place and thought. Some of the indignation faded from her expression. Somewhat hopefully, she said, "We don't know any Chicago detectives."

"I do," Branden asserted.

He excused himself, climbed the carpeted stairs to his study on the second floor, and came down holding a business card.

The Smiths were standing close together at the front door. He handed over the business card and said, "Get in touch with Bill Keplar. He's a good PI, and you can trust him."

The Smiths studied the card, and Denny slid it into his shirt pocket. As he opened the front door for his wife, Smith said, "Somebody's going to pay for our Brad. Somebody's sure gonna pay."

9

Thursday, August 10
8:00 A.M.

BRANDEN heard the sirens early Thursday morning, while standing at the kitchen sink eating cold cereal. Out of curiosity, when he drove off the college heights in the east end of town, he swung hard right onto Route 62 and drove slowly eastward. Soon he found water spilling onto the highway from one of the country driveways. A hundred yards farther down the road, he took in a startled breath and turned to climb the long, curving blacktop drive to Britta Sommers's house on a wooded hill.

The tires of his truck splashed through a steady flow of running water on the drive, and he could see dark smoke and billowing steam ascending beyond the stand of pines that blocked the view of her house from the road. As he came around the pines and made the turn at the switchback to her house, the firemen were coiling their hoses, pulling down hot spots, and extinguishing the last flames at the back of Sommers's sprawling brick ranch house, where a large kitchen with tall windows had previously offered a peaceful view of the woods on the hill behind the house.

Branden stopped and backed his truck into the trees beside the drive. He approached the house on foot and saw that the front was nearly untouched by the flames. At the side of the house, the fire had spread along the roof line and burnt to the peak. The back roof had been laid open by the blaze, and the back of the house was a shambles of sooted brick and charred wood, water dripping freely from the remains of the roof, the walls, and the door and window frames. At the back, all of the windows had been shattered either by the fire or by the firemen, and blackened wood, soot, and splinters floated on the water that was still running out of the house at foot level. The grass around the back of the house had been trampled to mud, and the flower beds beside the house were littered with charred boards, roofing shingles, ladders, high pressure hoses, and broken glass and window trim.

He could see that nearly all of the inside kitchen walls had been destroyed, as had those of an adjoining study at the back of the house. Only the upright studs remained, charred, with irregular patches of blackened wallboard hanging here and there in the ruins. The kitchen counters and cabinets had burned and canted inward, spilling their contents onto the rubble on the floor.

As he crossed the flagstone patio at the back of the house, Branden's feet crunched broken glass and splintered wood trim. Inside, he saw Captain Bobby Newell and the Millersburg fire chief working in the middle of the kitchen, painstakingly lifting boards, ceiling plaster, and sections of an interior wall from a long kitchen table that stood in the center of the room. He eased himself carefully through the back door frame and stood inside the sooty room to survey the damage.

Newell ushered Branden out onto the back patio and asked, "What do you smell, Professor?"

Branden, somewhat dazed, turned to Newell and asked, "What? What did you say?"

"What do you smell?"

"Smoke," Branden said, puzzled.

"No. It's out here, mostly," Newell said. "Smoke and burnt wood inside, where the fire was hottest, but what do you smell out here?"

Branden shrugged.

Newell bent over, picked up a tatter of window curtain, and held it to his nose. Then to Branden's nose.

"Gasoline," Branden said, frowning.

"It's all over out here, where the initial burst scattered all this glass."

"Arson."

"Exactly."

"I'm praying, Bobby, that the next thing you tell me is not that you found Britta Sommers in there."

"She's not there, Mike. Not at work, either. And we can't raise her on her cell phone."

Branden said, "I didn't notice whether or not her car is parked out front."

Newell nodded, "It is," and Branden groaned, clasped his fingers on top of his head, and dropped into one of the wet patio chairs.

10

CAL Troyer went looking for the professor late that afternoon on the campus of Millersburg College and found him in the firearms restoration labs in the darkened basement of the Museum of Battlefield Firearms. Branden was perched on a tall stool in front of a workbench on the far wall. There were two intense work lights trained on the work surface, which was covered with a thin rubber mat. Laid out on the mat were the sundry parts of an antique firearm. Branden was scrubbing meticulously with a toothbrush, cleaning the trigger group on a long gun. The gray metal parts and the brown wood stock were arranged in roughly the same order on the mat as they would take when the piece was fully reassembled.

Cal descended the steps, crossed the large, darkened room to Branden's workbench, and asked, "You got time to talk, Mike?"

Without looking up from his work, Branden said, "Hi, Cal," a weary tone in his voice.

Troyer stepped into the light of the workbench and leaned on his elbows to inspect the separate parts of the rifle. "Got someone's old rifle in the mail again?" he asked.

"Came in last week," Branden said as he worked.

"Civil War?"

"No. Pre–Civil War. More like the Black Hawk Wars. It's a breech-loading Hall. Made at Harpers Ferry in the 1830s."

Cal picked up the gray metal bayonet, fiddled with it absently, put it back in place, and said, "Lawrence Mallory told me you were down here."

"I didn't know Lawrence was in today," Branden said. He finished with the trigger group, set the works down, and turned on his stool to face Troyer.

"Are you working or thinking?" Cal asked, leaning sideways with his elbow on the bench.

"I like thinking down here. Quiet."

"I understand you're helping the sheriff with the buggy wreck out at John Weaver's place," Cal said. He pushed away from the workbench and stuffed his large hands into the back pockets of his jeans. He wore a plain white T-shirt that fit snugly over the muscles of his chest and arms. There was a carpenter's knife strapped to his belt. He was short and stocky, with large round eyes set far apart.

"Robertson's burnt up pretty bad, Cal. You been to see him yet?"

"Several times. I'm going back over tonight. They waved me off this afternoon."

"I've been going over as much as I can," Branden said. "Sometimes late at night when there are only nurses around. They let me sit in his room, but Bruce is wiped out. Can't really talk." After a thoughtful interval, Branden asked, "What do you think? Is he going to be OK?"

"There's a bit of infection. Mostly, I think he's tired himself out. At any rate, Missy Taggert has nurses posted at his door, and they're not letting anyone in this afternoon."

"They didn't expect he'd just lie still, did they?"

"Robertson?" Cal said and chuckled.

"I hear you've got Bruce on a prayer chain."

"Yep."

"You think he's that bad off?"

Cal laughed. "I think he warrants prayer in general, twenty-four/seven."

"It's serious, Cal," Branden scolded mildly.

"I know," Cal said softly. "You get that from watching Missy Taggert's eyes."

"Has she told you anything?"

"Nothing specific. I'm just not prepared to lose him without a fight."

"I'm not prepared to lose him at all," Branden sighed.

"I know," Cal said, his tone conveying a delicate veil of comfort, given sincerity by the lifelong friendships the three men had labored to preserve.

Cal tilted his head back, ran his fingers through his white locks, gazed again at the rifle at the table, and asked, "What's going on with the Weaver case?"

"It's not just Weaver anymore. There's Britta Sommers, now, too."

"Britta?"

"You haven't heard?"

"Been out with the Melvin P.'s all day."

"They're a Yoder sect?"

"Melvin P. Yoder. One little group that split off from a larger group so they could have phones in their barns several years back."

"Britta Sommers's house was torched this morning, Cal."

Cal whistled, surprised.

Branden added, "Nobody has been able to find her, either," and eased down from the work stool. The two climbed up the steps, circled around the lobby of the museum, and came out onto the lawn in front of the history building. They took seats on a bench under an old, split-trunk silver maple, and Cal said, "You think John Weaver's accident is connected to the Sommers arson?"

"She was trustee for his estate," Branden said. "He was what could best be described as a land speculator. Awfully good at it from what I can tell."

Cal frowned and said, "It's Weaver's land deals that brought me here to see you." Branden turned sideways on the bench to face Cal directly, interested in the apparent coincidences. Cal added, "It's going to ruin some farms in Melvin Yoder's sect."

Branden said, "I thought old man Yoder died a year ago."

"He did. They've got themselves a new bishop now. John Weaver's brother, from Pennsylvania."

"Andy Weaver?"

"So, you remember."

"Andy Weaver preached against the occult when it moved into Holmes County," Branden said.

"We both did. Now he's staying at Melvin Yoder's old place out in the Goose Bottoms. His family hasn't settled everything back home. They're to move out here, toward the end of the summer."

"His brother, J. R., used to be a member of the Yoder congregation."

"Loosely," Cal said. "He had pretty much quit on them in recent years."

"That would explain some of the things I saw out at his house," Branden said.

"Like what?"

"Telephone, computer, fax machine."

"That was all allowed in Melvin Yoder's sect," Cal said, "if it was a requirement for a home business. Won't be, now, with Andy Weaver in charge."

"He'll split them up," Branden said.

"Could be," Cal said. "There's at least one family who wants to keep their land and their phones and join a liberal group, up north of Trail. But the Walnut Creek bunch, starting out near the Goose Bottoms and west and north of there, are sticking with Andy Weaver. Taking down phone lines and selling off electric stuff like phones and faxes. They plan to keep a few electric lights in some of the district's shops and factories, because it's safer than oil lamps. But the rest of them are going back to wood stoves, kerosene lanterns, and plain black dress."

"Very unusual," Branden said.

"Andy Weaver is a very unusual man," Cal said dryly.

"He'll move against the cult, Cal."

"Eventually. Once he knows more."

"Does he know about the robberies I'm working, by Amish kids in goat's-head masks?"

"Yes," Cal answered flatly.

Branden eyed Troyer. "Is he prepared to be any help to me on that?"

"In time."

"He's got something more pressing?"

"Land swindles."

"Land?"

"Land swindles. Your John R. Weaver, no less."

"Back to the land baron," Branden said and wondered how Britta Sommers fit in.

"It doesn't affect the whole outfit," Cal said. "But Andy Weaver, the new bishop, takes the position that anything that threatens the well-being of one family threatens the well-being of them all. As it is, seven or eight young families are directly affected. John R. Weaver was going to terminate their farms on an obscure clause in their lease-to-own contracts."

"Can't believe Amish would go lease-to-own on land," Branden said, an eyebrow raised.

Cal said, "It goes back to Melvin Yoder, again. He allowed some of the younger fellas, starting out, to acquire their farmland from John R. on a lease-to-own basis. They're about halfway done on the payoff, and Weaver wrote them each a letter saying that he had decided to sell the land outright, for development."

"The way Britta Sommers explained things to me, he has already sold the land," Branden said.

"That's what Andy Weaver wants to talk to you about."

"Me?"

"Yes," Cal said. "Tomorrow morning, if you'll be free. I told him you would be."

"Just like that, Cal?"

"Have you forgotten how pleasant this county used to be before the big housing developers and the tourist industries took over, Mike?"

"I've got enough to do with the sheriff's office. First, there's Weaver's accident. Then Britta Sommers's house, and before that, riding decoy to catch those kids holding up buggies."

"Figured you would say that," Cal said and grinned. "I've got a little something that'll put you out at Bishop Weaver's place early."

"Is that a fact?" Branden said, amused.

"It is, Professor, and I'll tell you why."

Branden made an expression of exaggerated resignation and said with a growing smile, "Go on."

"One of Weaver's families has a son, gone English, who has worked as a surveyor for Jimmy Weston on some of these new, pricey, housing developments that are going up for rich city folk who want a place in the country. He's pretty much gone off the deep end. Crying mostly, and pounding his head with his fists, until they restrained him. He's been muttering strange things about John R. Weaver's dead buggy horse."

11

Thursday, August 10
6:55 P.M.

WHEN Branden arrived that night at Bruce Robertson's room in Pomerene Hospital, he found Dan Wilsher and Ricky Niell waiting outside in the hall. Robertson's door was open, and Branden could see Cal Troyer and Captain Bobby Newell inside. A nurse stepped away from her station in the hall and reminded Branden that the sheriff could have one visitor at a time, and then for five minutes only. When she spotted both Troyer and Newell in Robertson's room, she marched in authoritatively, scolded Robertson, and chased both men out of the room. Outside again, she laid down the law for all five of them.

When she had returned to her station, Captain Newell said his good-byes and left.

Niell said to Wilsher, "Is it still two days and then off the case, Lieutenant? Doesn't give us much time to figure out how Phil got caught in that pileup."

Branden said, "I think you're going to find that Weaver's accident and the arson out at Sommers's place are related. That gives us all the time we want, Ricky. Working on the one case means working on the other, too."

Lieutenant Wilsher said, "There's nothing material to connect the two."

"Sommers was John Weaver's trustee," Branden offered.

"That's more of a connection than you may realize," said Troyer.

"Your land swindles?" Branden asked.

"Right," Cal said and then explained for Niell and Wilsher that John Weaver had backed out on property lease-to-purchase contracts, apparently putting eight Amish families off their farms.

Niell commented, "Amish don't do lease-to-own."

Troyer answered, "It's rare, I'll grant you that. But we've got eight real cases, clustered in Melvin P. Yoder's old district."

Branden glanced in at Robertson and saw him struggling to rise up from his bed.

"That seems plausible," Wilsher said. "Sommers and Weaver, connected on the land aspect, I mean."

"Has anyone seen Sommers?" Troyer asked.

"We've been looking," Wilsher answered.

Branden watched Robertson and grimaced. He turned back to the group and said to Wilsher, "Dan, why don't you go in first. I think the sheriff is wearing out."

Cal said he had finished his visit and left. Niell and Branden waited while Wilsher made his report to the sheriff.

Niell glanced anxiously at his watch and said, "Ellie's expecting me."

"You still need to see Robertson?"

"Yes," Niell said, and drew a small spiral-bound notebook out of his hip pocket. "I've brought my notes."

Branden studied the little notebook in Ricky's hand and asked, "Has anything else happened that I don't know about?"

Niell thought. Tentatively, he said, "Got a visit from Brad Smith's parents. They asked to photocopy all of my notes."

"They paid me a visit, too. Did you give them your notes?"

"No."

"I told them to hire a private investigator in Chicago," Branden said.

Ricky nodded.

Niell went in when Wilsher came out, and Branden waited

in the hall alone. When Niell came out, Branden slipped into Robertson's room, closing the door.

Robertson lay on his back, eyes closed. He was sweating and looked exhausted to Branden. The professor stepped into the small bathroom, ran cool water onto a facecloth, squeezed it out, came back to Robertson's side, and used the cloth to dab at the perspiration on the sheriff's forehead and cheeks.

Robertson opened his eyes and said, "Thanks, Mike," taking the cloth and holding it to the side of his neck.

"Shall I call the nurse?" Branden asked.

"Just get me that nosepiece for oxygen."

Branden took down the clear plastic tubing that hung on the bed rail and slipped the elastic band over the sheriff's head. The two small ports he fit into Robertson's nostrils, and the sheriff lay still for several minutes, drawing deep breaths through his nose, while holding the damp cloth to his forehead.

When his breathing was relaxed again, Robertson dropped his arm to his side, and Branden took the cloth and hung it on the side railing where Robertson could reach it again.

"Couldn't be a worse time," Robertson whispered.

"Let Newell handle matters," Branden said.

"Newell doesn't give me as much detail in his reports as Kessler does."

"Ellie tells me Kessler's out on vacation."

Robertson nodded, closing his eyes momentarily.

"Niell and Wilsher will do just fine," Branden said, taking a seat in an overstuffed green chair, upholstered in smooth plastic.

"Niell should have made sergeant by now, but doesn't seem to care," Robertson said, gaze focused on the ceiling. "You gotta wonder about that. And Armbruster is just a rookie. So I want you working the Weaver case, too."

Branden said, "I've already got that worked out with Bobby, and Niell's better than you make him out to be, Bruce."

Robertson closed his eyes again, grunted softly, and brought his knees up with considerable exertion.

Branden asked, "What'd you get from Wilsher?"

"Says Britta Sommers didn't show at the bank. Hasn't been seen since yesterday."

"Has he got anything new from the Weaver place?"

"Been through most of the documents there, and some of the computer records," Robertson said weakly, eyes fluttering shut.

Branden eased the big sheriff's knees down to the bed and said, "Weaver's most recent land deals were with an outfit up in Cleveland. He and Britta Sommers had a corporation for land and other real estate matters."

Robertson nodded with his eyes closed.

"There weren't any papers, Bruce," Branden said, "but the last entries Weaver had made in his computer seemed to involve Holmes Estates up in Cleveland. Corroborates what Britta told me yesterday, and a buck will get you ten that Cal Troyer's problem with his Amish friends' land swindles is connected to Sommers's disappearance."

"What kind of land swindle?" Robertson asked, eyes open again.

"I'm not sure. We're going out there tomorrow."

"I thought you were never going to get over her," Robertson's voice trailed off.

"Ancient history, Sheriff," Branden said, but Robertson's eyes had closed.

12

Friday, August 11
7:06 A.M.

BISHOP Andy R. Weaver was rocking on Melvin Yoder's old front porch, smoking a pipe and waiting for Cal Troyer and Mike Branden. He had assembled the men an hour earlier and had cautioned them what could be said, and what could not. It was one thing to talk with English about their land troubles, quite another to mention the rest.

When he saw Branden's truck raising dust on the lane, he got up from his rocker and stood at the top of the steps of the porch. In spite of the heat, he was dressed in conservative Amish attire, high-lacing work boots, shiny blue jeans with baggy side pockets, brown cloth suspenders, and a dark blue shirt, the sleeves rolled up to his elbows. His vest was off, hanging on the rocker behind him. Beside the house, there was a line of buggies, the horses hitched to a fence that ran along a field of withered corn.

Branden and Troyer came up the steps, and Cal introduced the professor. Weaver offered his hand, and Branden shook it lightly, as he knew the custom to be so often among the Low Ones.

Weaver explained that the rest of the men were waiting inside, and he escorted the visitors into a front sitting room, where a dozen or so men sat on wooden benches lining the four walls of the room. They were each dressed to match the bishop, the only differences being the colors of a few blouses, one white, another light green, some pink. The rest were dark blue like the bishop's. All were handmade and buttonless, with a slit at the neck, running down about six inches, and tied with a string. As they sized up Troyer and Branden, there were soft murmurings in low German dialect.

The bishop clapped his hands to get their attention and instructed that they would all now use only English, for the benefit of their guests. Shaker chairs were provided for both Troyer and Branden, and the bishop offered a teapot and two porcelain cups, saying, "We are all having tea this morning."

Branden and Troyer each took a cup and waited for the bishop to begin.

The bishop said, "So that you will understand, Professor, I'll start by saying that my brother was a scoundrel and a cheat. He was a shepherd who fed only himself. He was right out of the Book of Jude. A 'cloud without rain, blown along by the winds'; an 'autumn tree, without fruit and uprooted—twice dead.'

"Money and land were his undoing. He loved both, to the exclusion of everything else. He also loved the modern and profane things that money can buy. He was dead to us long before the accident took his life, and all the troubles that are now about to befall us are the direct result of his greed.

"And Bischoff Melvin P. permitted him to remain in the district, because Yoder was too liberal. More liberal than any I have known, here or in Pennsylvania. I judge that he, too, was a vain and proud man, unwilling to exert his authority to cast my brother out of the fold. As a result, people like my brother were tolerated, loosely, in the congregation.

"Well, John Weaver should have been removed from the people long ago. They should have been allowed no dealings with him for land, or anything else, so far as I see it. But land was tight, and the district was growing, so Yoder allowed some of the younger fellas to acquire land a while back from my brother, on a lease-to-own basis, with no down payments."

Weaver gave both Branden and Troyer a copy of the lease-to-purchase contracts that John Weaver had used to set up the land transactions. Branden leafed through his copy and then decided he could do a more thorough job of reading it later. Cal started reading Clause A, and was interrupted by Andy Weaver.

Weaver said, "There was no trouble until two weeks ago. But the way I read that contract, there was bound to be trouble, sooner or later, and Bischoff Yoder should have seen it coming. Now, some of our families stand to lose their farmlands." He said something further in dialect, and eight men sheepishly raised their hands.

Branden said, "I'd want to look at this in some detail, later, and perhaps have a lawyer take a look at it, too."

Weaver nodded and said, "That's what I had hoped."

Then Weaver produced two copies of a letter. "Eight of our men received these letters almost two weeks ago."

Branden and Troyer read their copies of the letter, and when finished, Troyer whistled softly and shook his head. Branden opened his copy of the lease-to-purchase agreement and began to read Clause F.

"Can he do that, Professor?" one of the men asked from a bench.

Branden read the clause, and then the letter, again. When he had finished, he said, "I don't know. It appears so. Still, I can't be sure. This whole thing might hinge on how Weaver's trust is executed. Whether or not the buyback that Weaver intended is honored, and that may depend on who Weaver's inheritors turn out to be."

Branden turned pensive. He wondered, nervously, what it was that Britta Sommers actually had done. As if to assuage his concerns, he thought of her unquenchable spirit in high school. He thought of the college years when they had lost track of each other. He saddened, remembering the abusive years before her divorce had set her free. Now, it seemed, was the season of her triumph, cashing out to retire comfortably at forty-nine. But the fire changed everything, he realized, as did this matter concerning the land she had helped to sell. Eventually he spoke to Andy. "At the worst, if your brother had already cut the checks to buy you all out, and if he had actually also sold the land to someone else, maybe a developer . . . " He let the sentence trail off.

"How would we know that?" Andy asked.

"We've got to start with the bank," Cal said. "Unless Britta Sommers turns up, someone will be put in charge of John's trust."

Branden said, "Britta told me she had already transferred all her accounts to other officers. We need to know who took over J. R. Weaver's trust."

Andy said, "Are you saying that we may be able to keep the land, already?"

"I don't know just yet," Branden said.

"The boys have settled their families here," Andy said. "They've taken responsibility for a piece of God's land. They've paid both principal and interest, faithfully. Now, from what you are telling me, the land may already have been sold."

Branden rose from his chair and said, "We're going to try to stop that." He offered his hand to Weaver.

Cal rose and shook the bishop's hand, too. Now all of the men were on their feet, talking in dialect again, looking almost optimistic.

Bishop Weaver spoke a Dutch phrase to the men and followed Cal and Branden out onto the front porch. Branden went down the steps, but Cal turned to face Weaver.

"I lost another family, Cal," Weaver said.

Cal nodded sympathetically.

"And those two boys?" Weaver added. "It looks like the worst kind of trouble you could imagine."

"What do you plan to do about 'em?"

"I've got to confront them, Cal. Get them away from their parents and confront them face to face."

"That serious?"

"It's deeply spiritual, Cal, as you know. It may be worse than either of us could have guessed."

Cal said, "Whatever you need, Andy," and shook Weaver's hand.

"Don't tell Branden, Cal," Weaver whispered and turned back into the house.

On the ride home, Branden asked, "You said there was a boy from this congregation who's been acting strange?"

"He's not exactly a boy," Cal said. "He's twenty-four."

"Were any of his family at our meeting just now?"

"His oldest brother," Cal said. "He's one of the eight who stand to lose their farms."

"We need to talk to that family, Cal. Also the young man. If I can make arrangements to talk to him, can you set something up tonight with the family?"

"Who do you want to talk to?"

"His parents, first. Others if necessary."

Branden parked his truck in front of Troyer's white frame church house, and the two sat and read the lease-to-purchase agreement that eight young men had signed nearly thirteen years ago. There was a standard payment schedule, $80,000 over twenty years, at 8 percent interest, with no down payment. There was a clause that allowed the Amish to pay off the land after fifteen years. And there was Clause F, stating that if the value of the land should triple during the lease period, John R. Weaver could exercise the option to pay back the principal, plus a straight 8 percent interest, and then sell the land outright, to whomever he pleased.

13

BRANDEN found the offices and workrooms of the Weston Surveying Company in one of the old, spacious homes that line the Wooster Road in the north end of Millersburg. He parked in the rear lot, off an alley, and climbed the weathered steps to a wraparound porch. A hand-lettered sign beside the back screen door read "Weston Surveying—Please Step In" and gave the business hours. Branden rapped on the wooden door, pulled it open on noisy hinges, and stepped into a large room with faded wallpaper and high ceilings, trimmed in dark wood, with an aged metal desk and a battery of gray filing cabinets lining the walls.

He called out, "Hello," and heard a vague response from a room at the front of the house. He walked down a hallway and turned a corner into what had once been the foyer of the grand Victorian house. The floors were wooden, worn in places and covered in rugs elsewhere. The ceilings and corners were trimmed lavishly in wood. The hallways and smaller rooms of the house were cluttered with bins and boxes, map tables and charts, padded cases for surveyor's instruments—old Theodolites and the newer Total Stations with infrared beams and on-board computers. Tripods and prism poles were stacked in corners. Filing cabinets and computer stations of several varieties were positioned throughout the first-floor rooms.

In a small parlor at the front of the house, Branden found a diminutive, middle-aged man with curly blond hair, sitting on a rolling desk chair, pulled up close to a computer screen.

Branden stood in the doorway and waited with his badge holder looped over his belt in front.

The man's gaze remained fixed on the computer screen. He waved an arm to acknowledge the professor, said, "Be right with you," finished a few lines with a flourish at the keyboard, and spun his chair around to look up at Branden. He saw the reserve deputy sheriff's badge, stood up, offered his hand, and said, "I'm Jim Becker. Foreman."

Branden introduced himself and said, "I was hoping to find Jim Weston."

"Jimmy Weston is down to New Philly." Becker lifted a stack of magazines and charts from an old swivel chair and rolled it out for his visitor. Easing back into his own chair, he said, "Jimmy left a message on our machine last night. He's off on business. Said he'd be gone all day, maybe tomorrow, too."

Branden hesitated, wondering briefly if he should stay, and then took a seat. "So he might not be back for a couple of days?"

"Could be," Becker said. "You here about the wreck, or Britta Sommers?"

"The wreck," Branden said. "Weston evidently saw it all. Did he talk much about it?"

"Couldn't talk about anything else all day Tuesday," Becker said.

"I wanted to get his account of it," Branden explained.

"Jimmy's awful shook up," Becker said.

"About the wreck?"

"That and Brittany Sommers being missing."

Branden nodded and said, "They used to be sweethearts back in high school."

Becker pulled closer and said, "Jimmy still loved her," with an eyebrow raised. "She helped him out of a jam or two over the years."

"You're not his partner?"

"Foreman. He and I are the only two licensed surveyors in the outfit, and then we've got a crew of two more men who go out with us in two-man squads."

"But you did talk with him about the wreck?" Branden prodded.

"On Tuesday," Becker said. "We were supposed to finish up a couple of lots out north of Walnut Creek, but Jimmy couldn't work. Or so he said. By noon, I'd heard about all I cared to hear on the Weaver wreck, so I took the new guy out for a training run."

Branden gave a questioning look, and Becker explained.

"Since Larry Yoder hasn't been working—he's the fellow who used to hold prism poles for Weston—we've been short a man. We always need one to take data at the tripod and another to handle the prism rod."

"How long has that been?"

"Since we lost Yoder?"

"Right."

"Couple of weeks. Weston finally had to let him go officially. Wasn't reliable. Jimmy tried to help him, but Yoder was a nut case, and he wouldn't take his medicine. Had a drinking problem, too."

"The bishop out with the Yoder family said Larry Yoder was upset about some of the surveying you were doing," Branden offered.

"I reckon he was," Becker said, and eased back on his swivel chair. "We finished up on some five-acre tracts in the hills north of Walnut Creek for Sommer Homes, but Yoder got angry about something when we started in on the farms out there. You never know with that kid, anyways. He and Weston had words, and Yoder went off the deep end. I've seen him that way before. He blows hot and cold. One month he'll be down, brooding, and another he'll be pumped. Either way his temper gets the better of him and Jimmy fired him. Can't say as I'm sorry."

"From what I've heard, your Larry Yoder was upset that those farms were being cut up. He's got family out there."

"That's John Weaver's deal. Or it was. We just do the surveying," Becker said, somewhat defensively. "Anyway, Jimmy has put it all on hold, now that Weaver is dead and Brittany Sommers is missing."

Branden considered that and asked, "You say Weston is over in New Philadelphia?"

"Yes. Trying to scope out new surveying deals. That's a fresh area for us."

"Let's go back to what he told you about the wreck," Branden suggested.

"More than I wanted to know. Got so as I felt guilty that I wasn't out there myself. He even called me from the roadside after it happened."

"I probably saw him make that call," Branden said, remembering the chaos of the accident scene.

"He told me everything. It was like he couldn't shake the thing. There was a backfire, and the horse went down. Buggy stalled. Semi came over the hill too fast. Air brakes squawking and hissing. The jackknife. Cab crashed into the buggy and the trailer overturned on a car as it skidded on down the hill."

"That sounds about right," Branden said and stared at the carpet, thinking about the crash. After a moment, he thanked Becker, saw himself out the back door and sat for several quiet minutes in his car, wondering if there was any point in talking to Becker again. It surely was Weston he needed to talk to, but maybe not. There would be MacAfee this morning, and then the facts of the crash would be well established. Briefly, he wondered what had happened between Sommers and Weston after he had left high school for college. Eventually, he walked back into the offices, hunted up Becker and asked, "Do you know if Weston has been, well . . . 'involved' with Sommers lately?"

"Couldn't tell you," Becker said and shrugged. "He never talks much about that sort of thing."

The phone rang, and Becker wheeled his chair over to the desk. He said, "Hello," listened for a moment and said, "How in the world did you manage that, Jimmy?" Then he grinned, gave a laugh, and waved Branden farther into the room. At intervals he said, "I'm NOT laughing. Which hospital? All right. Sure, we can work south of Walnut Creek instead. OK. You sure you're all right? No problem. What? Nobody knows, Jimmy; she hasn't turned up. What? Right. OK, bye."

When he turned to Branden, Becker was smiling again, almost laughing. He tapped fingers on his knee and said, "That was Jimmy Weston, there. He's got himself in an emergency room over in Dover. Fell off some boulders at a prospective site and cut himself all to pieces in a patch of wild raspberries along an old barbed-wire fence."

14

CAL Troyer bent over beside the three-story white frame house and turned on the water spigot for Andy Weaver, who held the open end of the hose down in a shallow irrigation ditch in the garden beside the house. The warm water from the attic tank ran the length of the hose, spilled out the end, and disappeared into the dry soil. Eventually, the soil began to darken with the water. Slowly, the dark patch moved forward in the trough between two ragged lines of beans.

Andy laid the end of the hose in the trough and ambled back to Cal. They came slowly around to the shaded front porch and took seats, side by side, on a deacon's bench.

What was left of a large garden covered a scant quarter-acre beside the house. Beyond the garden there ran a sagging line of grapes, the thick shoots hanging with stunted new growth from wire strung between old posts. Behind the garden, three small, matching red barns with rusted metal roofs stood baking in the morning sun. Beyond that, high above the barns, there stood a windmill on corroded metal stilts. The white vanes of the windmill turned slowly from time to time in a light, irregular breeze.

The tin roof of the white house was painted a fresh, brilliant green, and red brick chimneys sprang from the peaks on either end of the roofline. Beside the house, the driveway was made of baked, packed earth. It came up to the house past a fenced area for a billy goat, and a sturdy wooden bench set on the lawn, taking the weight of three fifty-gallon drums of heating oil. The billy goat was munching on the end of a hay bale in the shade.

The long clothesline in front of the house was hung with the bishop's recent wash, dark blue shirts, denim britches, and sheets and towels in faded colors. Scattered on the lawn, there were several old white stumps where trees had come down over the years.

A neighbor lady in an aqua dress, long white apron, and black bonnet came through the front screen door and past Cal and Andy, carrying another basket of the bishop's laundry out to the clothesline. At the side of the house, her two youngest boys had set up sawhorses and were working in the heat, pink shirtsleeves rolled up, to install white-trimmed aluminum replacement windows in a downstairs room. By noon, the mother and her sons would be gone, and another neighbor's buggy would wheel down the drive, bringing the bishop's lunch.

Cal leaned back on the deacon's bench and stretched his legs out. He took a handkerchief and ran it over his forehead and around his neck. He turned slightly to Weaver and said, "Losing their farms doesn't mean they'd have to leave your congregation, Andy."

"You should know better, Cal," Weaver said gently.

"They'll still have their homes and five acres. That's enough for a garden."

"It's not just the men, Cal. I've got to think of their families, too."

"They can take jobs. The way cottage industries are springing up around here, there are always going to be jobs for anyone who wants one. Furniture shops, sawmills, buggy factories, printing shops. You name it."

"And where would their farms be?" Andy asked.

"They'd earn a living. Lots of Amish have gone that way since the tourists started coming."

"To our ruin, I'm sure. Besides, I expect the tourists will disappear one day."

"Amish are popular now, Andy. You'll always have the tourists."

"We've been persecuted before, Cal, and we will be again."

"That's a stretch, Andy."

"We're already hearing from children's services that farming is too dangerous for the younger ones. They say there are too many accidents involving our children."

"That's not going to settle out for a long time, Andy."

"I expect the day will soon come when some government agent will want to tell us how to raise our children, lead our lives, or handle our livestock. I predict those tourists of yours will grow to be judgmental, the more they learn of our ways. The locals are already like that enough, as it is."

"Maybe true, Andy, but for now, the men could stay in the congregation and hold down jobs for a livelihood. They might have lost their farms, but they'll still be Amish."

"To live Amish has always meant to farm," Andy replied. "To live independently and farm the land. And if a man has no farm, then what will he leave to his sons? Jobs in the city? Thank you, no."

"There are plenty of young fellows working at jobs already," Cal said. He took a hand fan out of a pocket at the end of the deacon's bench and began waving it slowly in front of his face.

Andy did the same and said, "If a youngster takes a job, it is meant to be short term. So he can save enough money to buy his own farm. Then he can marry. Raise a proper family. Take responsibility for his own household. That's the proper role for Amish fathers. Without the land, there can be no family. Besides, I've seen firsthand what idleness can do in a youngster's life."

Cal held silence.

Weaver got up slowly, and Cal followed him to the garden. The bishop bent over at the hose and moved it to the next irrigation ditch among the shriveled beans. He turned his eyes to the stationary vanes of the windmill and said, "First day, lately, we haven't had some kind of a breeze. The wind has kept my attic tanks full, but if that stops, I'll lose the garden."

"Save water for washing and cooking," Cal said and squinted at the sun. "Can't remember a hotter summer."

"We can use a hand pump on the shallow well for cooking. It's the irrigation and the livestock I'm worried about. I suppose it'd be no trouble to rig a gas pump and a line to the pond out back, but that's going dry too, and the livestock need it worse than the garden."

"I saw one of your neighbors turning his fields under the other day," Cal remarked.

"Henry Miller," Andy said heavily.

The two walked to the nearest of the three barns and stood in the thin line of shade cast by the high roofline. Andy stood quietly for a spell, watching the water run from the end of the hose and disappear into the thirsty soil. In an almost offhand way, he eventually commented, "We'll not be able to stay here, Cal."

"That's not like you," Cal said.

"I can't let these eight men take jobs off the farm."

"Then hire a lawyer," Cal said.

"That's not the Amish way," Andy said. "We'll wait to see what Mike Branden can figure out with the lawyer. Maybe there is a way out."

"What makes you think that?" Cal asked.

"I've got to try, Cal. Otherwise, as bishop, the only other advice I can give those families, in good conscience, is to move. Take the money they get for their farms, and make a fresh start, in another state. Someplace where the land values aren't forcing families off their farms because of the taxes. Someplace where the tourists and the big home builders haven't overrun the county."

After several quiet minutes, Weaver drew Cal around the corner of the barn and whispered, "I found a rubber mask in a barn, Cal. A goat's-head mask."

"What do you want me to do?"

"When I've learned who all is involved, I'll come for you, Cal. Until then, pray."

"I'll be ready."

"I know, Cal," Weaver said. "I know."

15

THE long white buildings of MacAfee Produce stood on the south side of Route 39, just below the hilltop town of Walnut Creek, where the road starts its descent into the Bulla Bottoms. Here, Walnut Creek cuts a wide and low, fertile valley into the surrounding highlands, and in a normal year, the flats would have been planted in abundant strips of corn, wheat, barley, and alfalfa. This year, the bed of Walnut Creek had already been baked to hardened clay.

Branden swung his truck into the parking lot, and found Bill MacAfee hosing out the bay of a new truck. Branden displayed his reserve deputy sheriff's badge, and MacAfee held up two fingers, saying, "Two minutes."

Branden had already talked with Robert Kent, one of the three accident witnesses, after Becker at Weston Surveying. MacAfee was the third of Ricky Niell's witnesses.

When he had finished cleaning the truck, MacAfee stepped onto the cement loading dock and shook Branden's hand, saying, "We can talk in the office."

Inside, MacAfee's office was a clutter of overstuffed filing cabinets, loose papers, and computer printouts. Cast-off magazines, ashtrays, used Styrofoam coffee cups, and wall calendars of young women in swimming suits. In front of his black metal desk, there was enough room for two small office chairs and a dusty, glass-domed gumball machine. Branden moved magazines from one chair to the other and took a seat in the narrow space facing MacAfee, his knees pressed against the front of the black desk.

With MacAfee standing behind the desk, Branden said, "I'd like to ask you what you can remember about the wreck last Monday on 515."

MacAfee turned to a shelf beside his desk, ladled coffee grounds into the filter of a drip maker and said, "I don't imagine there's a thing about that wreck I'll ever forget. It's stuck in my head like a nightmare."

He took the carafe into the hall, filled it with water at an old drinking fountain, returned, and poured the water into the machine. He flipped the switch and sat down as the machine started its first grumblings.

Branden said, "I need you to go over it again." He took out a pen and a small red spiral-bound notebook.

MacAfee said, "Why not?" and started wiping out two old coffee mugs with a towel that had been lying under some papers on his desk. He set one mug at the front edge of his desk for Branden, eyed the dripping coffee maker, and said, "I came up last in line, while the buggy made its turn. There were four cars right behind the buggy. Well, one car and the sheriff's car up front, and then two pickups a little further back, waiting in line."

MacAfee stood up and poured an early cup of coffee for himself and then started to pour for Branden. Branden held his fingers flat over the top of his mug and said, "No thanks."

MacAfee sat down with his coffee, sipped at it, and continued. "Anyways, I thought I saw the horse buck a little, and then the driver had trouble gettin' him goin' again. Next thing I know, that semi's coming over the crest of the hill up ahead, and it tumbles across the road, and the cab hits that buggy. By then the deputy had his car in reverse, and when the semi hit the buggy, pieces went flying everywhere. Axles, wheels, splinters.

Something long and heavy hit the deputy's windshield. There were blankets, a briefcase, a battery, and torn bits of fabric. You name it, it all came flying out of that rig and started raining down all around. Guess it couldn't have taken more than a few seconds, and then it all lay there on the road where it landed. That's when I noticed the fire underneath the first car. That one was smashed and pushed back a ways on the pavement, before the trailer came to a rest. It got plenty bad after that. I just sat in my truck at first. Couldn't seem to move."

Branden said, "There wasn't anything you could have done."

MacAfee shrugged with resignation and sipped at his coffee, eyes down.

Branden asked, "Are you sure you saw the cruiser backing up before the truck came over the hill?"

MacAfee thought a moment and then said, "Yes," tentatively.

Branden said, "Something else?"

"Oh, I'm not sure, but I remember feeling the same way."

"What way?"

"Like I should have been backing up, too."

"Do you know why?"

"Nope. Just had an uneasy feeling before I saw the truck coming on. Did I tell you that when I came back to my senses, I had my truck in reverse?"

"No. You didn't mention that."

"Didn't remember it until now. But I did, so I must have been wanting to back her up."

Branden thought about the unlikely coincidence of two drivers throwing their transmissions into reverse, and asked, "Did you shift into reverse before or after the crash?"

"Don't remember," MacAfee said, looking puzzled. "It was our new truck, too. The gears are still stiff, so I would have really worked at it, to get her into reverse that fast."

Branden asked several more questions that confirmed the recollections of the other witnesses, and then he closed his notebook, thanked MacAfee, got into his pickup, and headed back up onto the Walnut Creek hill, driving past the new inn and restaurant, to John Weaver's house in the opposite valley.

All three men had told essentially the same story last Monday, he thought. Now two had affirmed their statements today, and Becker had described Weston's account. There had been a line of cars and trucks, waiting for the buggy to make its turn. A sound like a truck's backfire. A horse that gave out in the turn. Schrauzer's cruiser backing up. Backing up hurriedly, Robert Kent had said. The semi cresting the hill and already starting to jackknife. And the impact that sent the buggy flying, detached from the horse that lay mangled by the impact, pawing at the air beside the road.

16

BRANDEN found Ricky Niell in John Weaver's trophy-room office, clicking through pages of documents on Weaver's computer. Niell turned around when he heard the door open behind him and said, "Hi, Doc," while holding his hand on the mouse.

Branden said, "How are you doing, Ricky?" and pulled a rolling office chair up beside Niell. "Find anything in there?"

"Normal stuff," Ricky said. He adjusted the gray tie on his black uniform shirt and sat up straighter. "It's like I said earlier. The newest entries are on a land deal with Holmes Estates, in Cleveland. He's got all his notes and figures on the computer, but the contract is on top of that filing cabinet."

Branden rose, took several papers off the cabinet and sat back down. The top document was a land purchase agreement with Holmes Estates. The last page bore signatures in two columns, one side signed by officers from Holmes Estates, the other side for Sommer Homes, where there were lines for two signatures, first Brittany Sommers, and then John R. Weaver. Sommers had signed, but Weaver had not.

"I found those papers in a briefcase out beside the road," Niell said. "Funny how Weaver hadn't signed."

"He'd have signed other copies," Branden said. "There'd be

no hurry for him to sign his own copy." Then he asked, "What all's in the files he kept on Holmes Estates?"

"Mostly notes on the land sale, and some figures," Ricky said. "And some spreadsheets marked 'Lease-to-Purchase.'"

"Can you bring up one of those spreadsheets?"

Niell said it would take a minute, and Branden rose to let him work. His eyes traveled to the gun rack on the wall, and Branden crossed the room and idly studied the rifles there, and then some of the hunting photos on the wall.

After a moment, Niell said, "I've got those files now."

With Branden back at his seat, Niell selected a file from the active documents menu, and scrolled to the top.

"That's an amortization table," Branden said. He read from the screen. "Daniel P. Yoder. $80,000 at 8 percent for twenty years. That's exactly what I'm looking for." The entries in the table began twelve years before, and finished up after twenty years, when the deed would transfer to Daniel Yoder.

Branden took the mouse, scrolled to the present year, and found that Weaver had underlined one entry. It was under the column headed "Accumulated Principal," in the row for July: $30,934.21.

"Bring up another one," Branden asked.

Niell took the mouse, clicked on another file, and found a similarly underlined entry, for July of that year: $28,928.93. The contract had been initiated several months later than the first one.

Branden whistled and said, "I think I know what he was doing." He leafed through the Holmes Estates contract, and found a parcel similar in size to those they had found in the amortization tables. Then he opened the center desk drawer, found a small calculator, and began punching numbers.

"Let's say Weaver sold a tract originally for the $80,000, as on that first one we looked at. After twelve years, Yoder would have paid $30,934.21 in principal." Then Branden took the mouse, clicked back to the first spreadsheet and found another figure. "He would also have paid $62,079.03 in interest, so that's profit to Weaver, clear and free." Then Branden switched to the land sale agreement with Holmes Estates. "A tract like that just sold for $304,082.99." He worked at the calculator and said, "That's an increase of 380 percent over twelve years. Now, all he has to do is pay Yoder back his principal, $30,934.21, plus a straight 8 percent interest." Again he punched numbers and said, "Total of $30,934.21 plus $2,474.74, or $33,408.95. Now, with the interest Daniel Yoder paid out over the past twelve years, that gives us $62,079.03 minus $33,408.95 for the buy-back, or $28,670.08 in profit that Weaver figured to make just on buying the land back at a straight 8 percent interest. Now we figure the new selling price, and we have $304,082.99 plus $28,670.08, or $332,753.07 made on the whole deal."

Niell said, "Now figure what Weaver bought the land for."

"That'll be over in the drawer," Branden said. "Take a while to look it up. But, if we rough it out at, say, $60,000.00, that's a net profit of $332,753.07 minus $60,000.00, or $272,753.07 on the whole deal, start to finish. That's something like," punching buttons, "450 percent, roughly, over twelve to fifteen years, before taxes."

"No wonder he sold," Niell said, and leaned back in his chair, hands clasped behind his head, eyes trained on the screen.

"It gets better," Branden said. "There were eight parcels."

Niell's eyebrows rose high on his forehead.

Branden said, "Let's say they all pretty much went the same way as this one did. That's eight times $272,753.00, or something like 2.2 million, walking away."

Niell seemed flabbergasted. "I'm in the wrong business," he muttered.

As they sat together in front of the computer screen, contemplating a clear profit of 2.2 million dollars, Branden's eyes drifted to the file cabinet where land deals were crammed so tight into the folders of three drawers that it was difficult to pull a single folder loose from the others. And he began to wonder nervously what role Britta Sommers had played over the years in J. R. Weaver's land speculations.

17

THAT afternoon, Branden drove west on State Route 39 and merged with U.S. 62 at Berlin, joining the slow-paced tangle of commercial and tourist traffic that labored its way through the town like the cars on a roller coaster, clawing their way to the top of the first hill. For a stretch of about a mile, on both sides of the road, through the little roadside town of Berlin, there could be found every conceivable type of vendor of Amish goods and country crafts, ranging from the finest handmade quilts and grandfather clocks, going for thousands of dollars, to dime-store plastic trinkets and jewelry for the kids. Dried flowers arranged in wicker. Amish oak furniture. Coat racks with Shaker pegs. Dried goods and tack. Postcards. Restaurants. Religious books. Throngs of people in cars, or crossing the highway on foot. The town was so overrun, and the traffic so backed up, that to drive the single mile could easily take three-quarters of an hour.

Branden fell in behind a dump truck loaded with gravel and started the crawl westward through town. On his cell phone, he tried Cal Troyer's number at the church, and left a message on the machine. Next, he tried the number at the coroner's office in the hospital. He let it ring several times, but Melissa Taggert's answering machine did not pick up.

As he sat in the traffic, he remembered her first year in Millersburg. Elected county coroner, but considerably overqualified for the position. She held advanced degrees from Ohio State, first her M.D. and then a Ph.D. in forensic pathology. Directly out of school, she had worked for several years in the medical examiner's office in Cleveland, and then had moved to Millersburg. She could have gone anywhere, Branden realized, but she came to sleepy Millersburg because of the uncomplicated quality of life in Holmes County. She had settled for the life of a small-town coroner, trading the salary and the perks of a big-city job for the country life. She had responded to the same allure of down-home living that had inspired Holmes Estates to develop farmland, so that rich people from places such as Cleveland, Columbus, or Pittsburgh could put up half-million-dollar homes on five acres of hillside, overlooking the picturesque fields of an Amish neighbor's farm.

In time, she had built a decent morgue and laboratory in a basement corner of the hospital, and with the right kind of steady pressure on the county commissioners, she had even managed to upgrade her duties, to something more along the lines of a medical examiner. Now, after several years with Bruce Robertson's help, she had built what could be regarded as an excellent forensics lab, in a county where life could be as simple as an afternoon game of horseshoes.

Branden smiled and remembered what Robertson had extracted from her, in exchange for his help over the years—a guarantee of her support when it came time to move the sheriff's office out of the little red brick jail next to the courthouse and into a modern facility on a hillside north of town. Using his own money, Robertson had hired an architect in Wooster to render an artist's sketch of how the facility might look on the hill he had chosen near the County Home, and without making a noticeable point out of the matter, he had hung the drawing in his office in the red brick jail. When people asked about it, he would reply, "Just doing some dreaming, is all. Just a little dreaming."

When Branden pulled free of the traffic snarl in Berlin, he

continued into Millersburg on 62, circled the courthouse square, and parked one block north on Monroe Street. He walked into the county recorder's office, in an old converted grocery store, and at the front desk, he spoke briefly with the recorder. He took what he learned to one of the computer terminals and began a search for any land transactions involving Holmes Estates. After some effort, he concluded that no such transactions had been recorded.

Branden paused at the computer, thinking, aware now that neither Sommers nor Weaver had filed the land sale with the recorder yet. Then why not Holmes Estates? They should have filed by now. Another thing. Who would handle the transaction with Sommers missing and Weaver dead? Perhaps the new trustee of the Weaver estate. Would there have been copies of the land purchase agreement at Sommers's house? Or in her office at the bank? Why wouldn't the trust officer have filed on behalf of Weaver's estate by now? Why hadn't Brittany Sommers filed the papers herself?

At the front counter in the recorder's office, Branden found the recorder's assistant, an attractive, middle-aged woman, sorting papers at her desk behind the counter. She glanced up from her work, straightened the papers briefly, stepped to the counter, and said, "Yes?"

Branden said, "Mike Branden, working for the sheriff's department," and displayed his badge.

"You're that big professor up on the hill," she said and smiled genially.

Branden said, "Yes," blushed slightly as she continued to smile at him, and asked, "Can you tell me how long it usually takes to file a land sale?"

"It varies," she said. "Sometimes they bring it in right away. Sometimes it takes a week or more."

"I would expect this to be a big sale, and thought it would have cleared by now."

"The big ones get stalled in the map office," she said and

nodded her head in the direction of the map department, next door.

"But you get them all, eventually?" Branden asked.

"Every last little thing," she replied. "They all go into the computer the same day that we get them."

Branden thanked her and walked absently out of the building, wondering how big the Weaver/Sommers deal really was. He realized he and Ricky Niell had made only a rough estimate of the thing. As he crossed the street to his truck, he phoned the bank, inquired fruitlessly about Britta Sommers, and got the name of the trust officer who was now handling the estate of John Weaver. Once transferred to the right secretary, he made an appointment for 10:00 A.M. Monday. Leaning against his truck, he dialed Cal again at his church, and got him there on this try. As he slid behind the wheel and started the truck, Branden said, "Hi, Cal. Are we still on for tonight?"

Cal answered, "9 o'clock. I'll pick you up at your house, if that's OK."

"That'll be fine," Branden said. "You're the one who knows where we're going."

"I haven't seen Caroline in a while," Cal said. "Maybe I ought to come for dinner."

"She's not home, Cal. Been in Arizona with her mother. She won't be back for a while yet."

"Does she know about Bruce?"

"I call her every night."

"Tell her I said Hi."

"Sure thing. You still want to come for dinner?"

"I'm a better cook than you are, Professor," Cal said and gave a little chuckle.

"Then you bring dinner."

"I'll buy a couple of pizzas."

"That's what I thought. You say you can cook, but it's always carryout."

"Pizzas at seven, Mike."

"Pizzas at seven," Branden repeated, and switched off.

As he drove for Pomerene Hospital, Branden dialed Ellie Troyer on the front desk at the jailhouse. When she answered, he said, "Ellie, this is Mike Branden. Is Bobby Newell in?"

Ellie said, "I'll connect you, but have you heard about Sheriff Robertson?"

Branden said, "No, I've been out all day."

"He's worse, Professor. A whole lot worse from the way I understand it."

"What's wrong?"

"He's got an infection that they're having trouble with. Something about his antibiotics. Melissa Taggert is with him now. His doctors, too."

"I've been trying to reach her."

"She's been tied up with Bruce all day," Ellie said. "Anyway, I thought you would want to know. Here's the captain."

"Hello," Newell said, "Captain Newell."

"Bobby, it's Mike Branden. Have you heard anything from Britta Sommers?"

"No."

"It's not like her to have run off, Bobby."

"What can I say? Maybe she doesn't want to be found. She probably set fire to her own house, Mike. You ever think about that?"

"Good grief, Bobby, her place is all burnt to pieces, and she's missing. You really think she did that?"

"It's a theory."

"Well, it's not a very good one."

"So you say, Professor. Have you heard about the sheriff?"

"Ellie just told me."

"I think it's fairly serious."

"I'm driving over there now," Branden said, and switched his cell phone to the other hand. "In the meantime, I think you should reconsider the Sommers thing. Let's go out to Britta's place. See what we can find."

"Like what?" Newell said.

"I'd search through documents in her study. She's supposed to have signed an agreement on a land sale, and I need to know what else she might have signed before she disappeared."

"Her study is toast, Mike. We haven't been able to identify any documents at all. None in her desk and none in her filing cabinets."

"I thought they got the fire out quickly," Branden said and turned into the hillside parking lot of the small hospital.

"Whoever torched the place opened all of her drawers and doused all of the papers with gasoline before starting the fire," Newell said, as Branden pulled into a parking spot. "There aren't any papers left to look at."

Branden thought about the obvious importance of that as he got out of the truck and said, "I'd still like to look it over, Bobby."

Newell hesitated and then said, "I guess I don't see any problem with that."

"OK," Branden said, standing outside the emergency room doors. "I'll try to set it up for tomorrow morning."

"Not a problem," Newell said. "Let me know how Robertson is doing. By the way, did you know Missy Taggert pulled a .30-caliber bullet out of the left flank of Weaver's horse?"

Branden smiled in satisfaction and said, "I figured she might."

"You figured."

"Right. I asked her to take a look."

"That's a strange bit of figuring, Professor."

"I just had a hunch. Hey, look, Bobby. I'll come by as soon as I can and explain that to you."

Newell changed the subject. "You still going to work on those buggy robberies for us?"

"When I can," Branden said. "I figure Weaver and Sommers take precedence."

"You know, I called that ward in Nashville where her son lives. They haven't heard from her. We're also checking airlines and car rentals. And Mike, I've checked back through our records on the robberies those kids are pulling. Turns out it was our John R. Weaver who filed the first complaint, about nine months ago."

"Weaver was robbed by those kids?"

"He was the first we knew about. Took his whip to 'em and beat them off. He told us later that he was carrying twelve hundred dollars at the time. His report also states that he saw one of their faces. The kid was nervous and hot under his mask, and took it off. Weaver told us he could recognize the kid if he ever saw him again."

"Hey, I'll call you back. I'm going into the hospital now," Branden said and switched his cell phone off.

On the third floor, Branden found Melissa Taggert leaning against the door frame to Bruce Robertson's room, talking quietly with a doctor in a white coat. The doctor recognized Branden and said, "No visitors tonight, Professor."

Branden looked to Taggert, and she confirmed it with a brief nod of her head. She led him quietly by the elbow, away from Robertson's room, and they took seats in a small waiting room at the end of the short hall. Taggert had her long white doctor's coat on, with a stethoscope looped around her neck, and latex gloves on her hands. She snapped the gloves off, and then took a blue cloth face mask from her neck.

"It's the infection," she said, sitting on the edge of her chair. "There's been some trouble with his antibiotics line. His lungs are filling up with fluid, too, and the infection is a strain that is not responding to the normal protocols. I'm worried it may be a resistant strain. That means we have only a few antibiotics we can try, and for that, I'm going to transfer him to Children's Hospital in Akron. They've got one of the nation's best burn units there, and they take adult patients. They'll consult with an infectious diseases expert."

"When?" Branden asked.

"Tonight. We're using Life Flight out of Columbus," Taggert said, obviously worried.

"Why so soon?"

"It's a bad infection, Mike. If it gets into his blood, we won't be able to stop it. Even as it is, he'll need continuous IV treatments with antibiotics that still work on resistant strains. There aren't that many that still work."

"But that'll do the job, right?"

"I can't tell," Taggert said, a vast concern evident in her eyes. "I'll get him up there tonight. It'll take a day or two to run the cultures. Then, they'll start him out on the strongest antibiotics that his kidneys and liver can tolerate. It'll take time to run screens, but if his kidneys can't take the pressure, or if the strain is vancomyacin-resistant *Staph a.*, then it's not good at all."

"Are you saying he could die?"

Melissa looked steadily for a while into Branden's eyes and then turned her gaze down. After a quiet and awkward interlude, she whispered, "There isn't anything I wouldn't do for him."

Branden looked away momentarily and turned back to Taggert. "Akron is the best place for him?" he asked softly.

"I think so."

"What are his chances?"

Melissa looked down at her hands, folded lightly in her lap. The shadows of her eyes gave the look of quiet sorrow. She began to speak again, but couldn't. Her eyes grew moist, and she cleared her throat with difficulty. Then she looked into Branden's eyes and said, "You know we spend a lot of time together on the job."

Branden nodded, "Yes."

"He's a hard man to nail down."

"I know," Branden said and leaned forward, his face scant inches from hers. He whispered, "I also know, as well as anyone, Missy, that he'd be a hard man to love."

Melissa coughed a little, fought a constriction in her throat, and said, "Tonight or tomorrow, whenever he's first awake enough to talk, I'm going to make certain that he knows how I feel about him."

Branden didn't ask her to finish the thought. He didn't need her to. He knew it went something like, "because that may be the last chance I'll have to tell him."

18

Friday, August 11
9:20 P.M.

AS TROYER and Branden turned into the gravel drive at the Yoder farm, a floodlight out near the road illuminated stubby brown stalks of corn in the dry field that skirted the lane. Beside the lane, there was a small red building about the size of a one-seater outhouse, and a telephone line came into it from a pole out on the road. The temperature lingered near ninety degrees, despite the fact that the sun had slipped below the horizon. The last soft light of evening suffused a cloudless summer sky.

At the house, they stepped out of Cal's air-conditioned truck, and the dry heat assailed them. On the front steps, there was a teenager in Dutch costume, sitting alone with his ear bent low to a battery-powered radio. Cal spoke to him in dialect, and the boy vigorously shook his head, replied briefly, popped up, and darted around the corner of the house.

As they mounted the steps, Branden asked, "What was that all about?"

Cal said, "I asked him if he liked rock and roll."

"And?"

"He said he was just listening for the weather," Cal said, and laughed softly.

A young man with a wild look in his eyes burst through the screen door and grabbed Troyer's hand, pumping it rapidly up and down, shouting "Vie Gehts! Vie Gehts! Vie Gehts!"

He switched to Branden, grabbed his hand and forearm, and pumped it too. "Vie Gehts! Vie Gehts! Vie Gehts!"

Hannah Yoder came out in a rush and took hold of the man, wrapping her arms around him, pinning his hands to his side. "OK, Benny. That's enough, already." She seemed to bring him under control with her voice, and by rubbing softly on the top of his head, and then her husband came out and took Benny inside.

Hannah shrugged sadly and let them in. "Benny has a screw loose," she said, and led them into a large kitchen. "We have refreshments."

A single kerosene lamp sat glowing on a kitchen counter. In the center of the room stood a square cherry table with chairs for twelve. On the table, there was a cherry lazy Susan, almost half as wide as the table itself. The polished lazy Susan held a pitcher of water, two glasses, a bowl of chipped ice, slices of a fruit-nut bread, and apple butter in a canning jar. Two places were set with plain china, and the Senior Yoder curtly invited Branden and Troyer to "take seats, and help yourself." Then he walked into an adjoining pantry and tuned to a weather station on a little radio there.

Hannah Yoder, obviously embarrassed, followed her husband into the pantry, and the two began talking.

Cal shrugged, took a slice of the bread and laid on a thick covering of apple butter from the lazy Susan. Realizing that the conversation in the pantry concerned them, he whispered a translation for Branden.

"Dadscht du's laube, Crist?"

Will you permit it, Crist?

"Der bishop haut tzaud es ist gut."

The bishop has said it's OK.

"Des vher dau allebescht vague fah ein helfa."

This is the best way to help him.

"Hannah, der English Docktoro haut Larry nichts gut favischt."

Hannah, the English doctors have been no good to Larry.

"Aahr ist in druble, Crist. Favoss kenna meah net helfa?"

He is in trouble, Crist. Why can't we help him?

"Favoss tzellaama der Sheriff tza va ein?"

Why tell the sheriff about him, now?

"Larry braucht tzei medicine."

Larry needs the medicine.

"Aahr muss tzrich kumma un sa fasprechen nemma, ist alle."

He needs to come back and take his vows, that's all.

"Aahr braucht tzei medicine, Crist."

He needs his medicine, Crist.

"Est du tuscht ein mai drubble macha."

This will only get him into more trouble.

"Aahr ist uscht grangt. Der kupf Doctor in Wooster saught aahr braucht tzei medicine."

He is sick, is all. The psychiatrist in Wooster said he needs to take his medicine.

"Aahr nemtz net medicine. Vass kenna ma du?"

He won't take his medicine. So what can we do?

"Der Doctoro haut ein ferschlossa in da hospital in Canton. Aahr musst medicine nemma."

The doctors have him locked up in the hospital in Canton. He has to take his medicine, now.

"Cis net's medicine es aahr bracht."

It's not the medicine that he needs.

"Crist, Aahr ist fahudelt."

Crist, he's touched in the head.

"Aahr muss landschaffe. Aahr set bauede."

He needs to farm. Work the land.

"Es dad ken schaude du fada Professor saah vas meah vissa."

It won't hurt to tell the professor what we know.

Last of all, Crist Yoder said, "Aahr kumt vedda in druble mit der Sheriff," and walked outside. Hannah Yoder came back slowly into the kitchen and, a little flustered, took a seat opposite Branden and Troyer.

She said, "My husband doesn't understand about mental diseases."

Cal asked, "Will it be all right if you talk, now?"

Hannah said, "Shore. Crist just doesn't see what good it will do, already."

"I understand that Larry is at Aultman Hospital," Branden offered.

"Yes. We drove him there after Mr. Weston brought him home," Hannah said.

"How?" Branden asked.

"We used old Bishop Yoder's van," Hannah said. "He used to keep one, you know. He even had a driver. Now we just keep it at one of our houses, and people who need it can use it. Anyways, when Larry came here yesterday afternoon, he was crying and pounding his head with his fists. He was drunk real good, and he kept moaning about a horse. Anyway, our oldest son, Elmer, drives, so he got the van from a neighbor and drove us all to Larry's psychiatrist in Wooster. He told us to take him to Aultman. The emergency doctors there sent him up to the psychiatric ward, and we drove home. That's when we got your message off the machine out front."

Branden asked, "What was it he said about the horse?"

"Oh, I don't know. I don't suppose any of us could tell you, outright. Something about how sorry he was that the horse got killed. Or that he shot it. It didn't make too much sense. Mostly he mumbled, cried, and tried to hurt himself. Crist had to force a knife out of his hand when he started cutting his arms." She stared sadly at her fingers for a moment longer and asked, "Can you look in on him for us?"

Branden gave his assurances and asked, "Where did he cut himself?"

Hannah drew a finger several times across the outside of her upper arm and said, "Here."

"Do you know what his mental troubles are?" Cal asked.

"Manic-depressive is what they say."

"Is he on lithium?" Branden asked.

"Supposed to be," Hannah said. "But he drinks a lot. Mr. Weston has been trying to help him, but I don't think he's been able to do much good."

Branden asked, "Are you certain he only cut his upper arms? Not his wrists?"

"Just his upper arms," Hannah said. "Does that mean anything?"

Branden said, "People like Larry try to get the pain out that way. He probably wasn't trying to hurt himself badly. Not really trying to kill himself."

"He's tried that, already," Hannah said. "My husband is worried he's got a head like Benny. Crist has a brother in the mental house in Massillon, and he's afraid it's got into Larry and Benny, too. The doctors say it's the genetics."

Branden nodded his head slowly, wondering if there would ever be a chance to interview Larry Yoder himself.

"Why did the horse bother him so much?" Cal asked.

Hannah shrugged and said, "The horse just got stuck in his head, somehow. He'd be like that, sometimes. Couldn't stop thinking about things that troubled him."

Branden said, "I gathered that you spoke to your new bishop about this."

"Yes. Because Crist was so uncertain about calling you. We both went to see him. The bishop said we should tell you everything."

Cal helped himself to another slice of bread and apple butter, and Branden said, "John Weaver is tied up with your son somehow?"

"It's roundabout," Hannah said. "John used to be active in the congregation. Lately, he wasn't. But back when he was active, he helped several of the boys get started on their farms."

"Larry knew about that?" Branden asked.

"Oh yes. Everybody did. It was good, then. The young men got their land with no down payments."

"Are you aware," Branden asked, "that those lands are now being sold off for housing developments?"

"Our Larry told us that was going to happen, about a month ago. He was angry that John Weaver was tryin' to swindle people out here. Anyways, it was a good deal back then. John R. owned most of the land hereabouts, and our district was growing too fast. He sold at a fair price, and let the boys pay it off as they could. Our Elmer was one of them."

"They had leases, with options to buy after fifteen years," Cal said.

"We're coming up pretty close to that, now," Hannah remarked.

"And you haven't heard about Weaver's sell-off?" Branden asked.

"The bishop said something like that could happen, already. I won't believe that Amish would do that to Amish. Won't believe it until I see the sheriff out here movin' families off their land."

"You also said Larry seemed to know something about this, almost a month ago."

"He did."

"How?"

"Surveying, I guess."

"Surveying?"

"Larry worked for the Weston Company, as a surveyor."

"I was just out at Jim Weston's offices," Branden said. "They told me Larry got himself fired."

"It's true," Hannah said and sighed. "But, if you really want to know, it was Brittany Sommers's company. Larry told us Weston owned only 40 percent."

"Where was Larry surveying?" Branden asked.

"All around Walnut Creek."

"North?"

"North and south. He's been working the same areas for the last month or so."

"How do you know that?" Cal asked.

"Larry visited a lot," Hannah said. "Likes to take his suppers here. We all thought it was pretty strange work, but he said he was cutting out small tracts of land for houses over near Winesburg, and that he was supposed to start doing the same thing near Walnut Creek, pretty soon."

19

Saturday, August 12
8:45 A.M.

BRANDEN sat at his desk in his corner office on the second floor of the old history building at Millersburg College, reviewing the manuscript changes that his executive assistant, Lawrence Mallory, had penciled into their latest paper. Branden's desk was backed up into the angle in a corner of the office, where the oak-trimmed windows of two walls gave him a view of the commencement Oak Grove, with its tall oaks and distinguished maples. He laid the manuscript on his desk and turned his desk chair to face the windows. His gaze wandered across the lawns and the flower beds, where, each spring, his seniors celebrated after commencement, still not participants in the workaday world, but no longer simply college students, either.

After a few peaceful memories, Branden's eyes lost their focus on the scene below, and his mind returned to the puzzle of facts in the Weaver/Sommers cases. Time passed, and he let his thoughts, mere suspicions that flickered lightly into consciousness, carry him randomly through the case without the need or inclination to organize, sort, or ponder specific facts.

In time, Mallory spoke from his desk in a vestibule at the front of the office. "Doc," he intoned. "I don't think you're working on our manuscript anymore."

Branden swung himself away from the windows, took another page of the document, and tried to focus his thoughts on the soft pencil additions and corrections that Lawrence had made in a delicate hand. As with the other pages, each editorial suggestion Lawrence had made was sensible and helpful, improving the writing by adding a touch here and there of the smooth and graceful prose that Branden had learned, over the years, to expect from Mallory. If Lawrence had penciled something into the text, it was because it needed to be there. If he had taken something out, it was because it was superfluous.

Branden gathered the pages together, stacked them on edge, started across the room and said, "It all looks good to me, Lawrence."

"Did you read it all?" Lawrence asked, with mild insistence, from behind his desk.

"Almost everything," Branden said and smiled.

"Mike, sometimes I think . . . "

Branden interrupted. "It's all excellent, Lawrence. Everything. You know what we're after with this one."

Mallory laced his fingers together on top of his desk and said, "Hoped you would like it. Especially that new lead into our analysis of the action at Resaka."

"It's very fine, indeed, Lawrence," Branden said and dropped the pages onto Mallory's desk. "Make your changes and send it off. Let's try a different editor this time."

"Maybe Schoefield?"

"That'd be fine."

Lawrence took up the pages and arranged them fastidiously beside his computer. Without looking up, as he began work on the document, he said, "I see you've finished with the Hall carbine."

"It's a nice piece," Branden said. "Are we going to be able to use it, or should I send it back to the owner?"

"It'll go well in our early Civil War period."

"There weren't that many Halls in the Civil War."

"Enough," Lawrence said. "They were issued to the Eighth

New York Cavalry. The model 1843s were all over. First and Second North Carolina Cavalry, and Second Florida's, too."

Branden congratulated Mallory with a broad smile and a military salute and said, "Lawrence, you'll be having my job, someday."

"Just say the word," Lawrence quipped.

Branden laughed and strolled back to stand behind his desk. With his hands in his pockets, he studied the lawn outside his windows. Early as it was, the morning sun came in through the windows with the intensity one expects only in the Southwest. Branden, accustomed to the cool woodlands and cloudy skies of northeastern Ohio, squinted at the light, and thought of the drought that had settled onto the farmlands of the county. The temperature outside was climbing into the nineties again, and the glaring light made the professor nervous.

After a while, Lawrence stopped typing and said, "I hear you're working the Brittany Sommers disappearance."

"Also the Weaver murder."

"That wasn't an accident?"

"The coroner pulled a .30-caliber bullet out of the horse."

"Do you know who did it?" Lawrence asked.

"Can't say for sure," Branden said, "but Larry Yoder, an Amish fellow gone English, looks like a good suspect."

"That's the Larry Yoder up in the Aultman psych ward?" Lawrence asked.

"You know about that?"

"Gossip is king in this county, Professor."

"Well, then, yeah. Larry Yoder looks good for the Weaver murder right now." Branden added, "I've got to get out to Sommers's house now. Then there's still Larry Yoder to see, and Bruce Robertson later at the Children's Hospital burn unit in Akron. You sure you're all squared away on that paper?"

"No problem, Mike," Lawrence said. "If there's anything you

need, just let me know." Then Mallory added, "Larry Yoder might be a handful, Doc."

"You know something, Lawrence?"

"He's some kind of trouble, is all. Anyway, there are rumors."

"About the shooting?"

"No, earlier. Maybe he's out of it now, but back in his Amish days, Larry Yoder was into some foul stuff. At least that's what I heard at the time."

"Like what?"

"Something about rituals," Mallory said, with a distasteful expression.

"Good grief, Lawrence, he used to be Amish."

"It's just what I hear."

"I guess I'm not all that surprised," Branden said, and left, thinking of the obvious connection to two goat's-head masks.

At Sommers's house, Branden parked off the drive in the stand of pines where he had parked during the fire. There was a sheriff's black-and-white cruiser in the driveway, and Ricky Niell's distinctively large, black 4x4. Around back, Branden stepped over the scattered shards of glass on the patio and opened the back door to the kitchen. Inside, he found Dan Wilsher and Ricky Niell. Wilsher was using a Polaroid camera, and he had a 35 mm outfit strung back over his shoulder. Niell held an aluminum tripod, on top of which was an intense lamp. A battery pack for the lamp rested below, on a shelf within the legs of the tripod. The odor and sting of smoke was pervasive.

Wilsher snapped a shot of char patterns on what was left of an interior wall, and then swung the 35 mm camera around and took several more shots with a close-up lens, while Niell held the light on the spot. Wilsher pulled the 35 mm camera back over his shoulder, said, "Newell said you'd be coming out," and shook Branden's hand. "Not sure how much you can see. Electricity's been off since the fire."

Niell and the lieutenant were dressed in old work clothes and wore high rubber boots. Their clothes were sooted with black smudges from the burned timbers and blackened debris of the scene. Niell's hands were also black, and there were sooty marks on his face.

"The state fire marshal's office was out here yesterday and ruled it was arson," Wilsher continued. "Niell, there, can fill you in. Andy Shetler's on vacation, so I have to take these photos."

Niell followed Wilsher around the room, training the light on each area the lieutenant pointed out for a photograph.

To Branden, Niell said, "The fire chief and his crew will serve as expert witnesses that there was gasoline, a lot of it, on the scene, but I took some samples out of the floor crevices for Taggert. I guess she's got a way to test for gasoline."

"What do you mean by 'a lot of it'?" Branden asked.

"There's swirling char patterns everywhere," Niell said. "On the floors, the furniture, file cabinets, counters, and walls. There's also a trail of swirling burns outside on the patio, leading back toward the woods. The windows are blown out pretty uniformly. So, whoever it was pulled papers out of the filing cabinets in the study, doused them all, and everything else for that matter, opened most of the windows, poured himself a fuse out onto the patio, and touched her off from out there. The fumes had saturated the rooms, and when the fuse burnt to the door, the flames erupted almost everywhere, at once, blowing out the glass in the top panes. Then also, all the charring patterns, like alligator skins on the uprights, are fairly uniform, meaning the fire burned evenly, everywhere at once. There wasn't an identifiable point of origin."

Branden said, "You've done some studying, Ricky."

"Just got a lecture from the fire marshal, yesterday," Niell said. "Anyway, the marshal says it was torched by an amateur."

Branden's eyes questioned.

"He didn't pour a long enough fuse," Ricky explained.

Branden asked, "And how do you know the fire spread through gasoline that had been splashed all around? You said even on the walls."

"That was the fire marshal's call," Niell said. "There are two types of charring patterns on the walls. Some near the floor that burned up in a V shape. Then others higher on the walls, that burned in an inverted V shape. There was also thorough burning in all the open file cabinet drawers, and on all the furniture. Like the fire started all throughout the back two rooms, pretty much simultaneously."

Branden considered that as he followed Niell to a new location for a photograph and then said, "Who spotted the fire, Ricky?"

"A Millersburg cop. Bill Hadley. Coming in that morning for his shift."

"Did he describe the fire?"

Niell said, "He saw tall plumes of dense, black smoke, found the rear of the house engulfed, and called it in."

Branden said, "The black smoke fits with the gasoline."

They stepped over scattered debris in the kitchen and started taking pictures in the study. A wooden desk was charred and blackened, the desk chair blown over backwards onto the floor. The metal filing cabinets had sagged from the heat of the flames. The drawers, all opened, held tangled wads of burned and water-logged papers. Branden stepped to the drawers and found all of the pages blackened to the bottom, where thin white edges that had been protected from the heat stood out against the black at the top of the papers. Branden tried to lift several pages from various drawers, but they crumbled as he pulled on them. Giving up, he came back to Niell and watched the photographic work for a while.

After studying the debris that had been scattered by the

explosion, Branden said, "It looks as if stuff is blown in about every direction. Just scattered randomly. No apparent direction of blast."

Niell said, "The fire marshal said that happens with low-order explosions."

"This was a low-order explosion?" Branden queried.

"Yeah," Ricky said. "Compared to what you'd get with gunpowder or plastique."

Branden nodded, satisfied with what he understood now about the fire. He said, "I had hoped to search for some documents here."

Wilsher shot a Polaroid and stood up. "There's nothing left to see, Mike. Taggert has the papers that were laid out on the floor to burn, but there's little more than ash."

As Wilsher started to pack up his cameras, Branden asked, "Do you mind if I have a look through the rest of the house?"

Wilsher thought it over, said, "No," and added, "but take Niell with his light there. The department turned off the electricity during the fire, and all the curtains were pulled before the fire. I'd like them to stay that way for now, so the whole house is dark."

Branden passed through the kitchen and into the living room, Niell trailing with his portable light. "Sommers evidently isn't much of a housekeeper," Niell observed.

In the living room, laundry was piled on a sofa, and magazines were strewn across an end table and on the floor around the table. In the bathroom, the medicine cabinet was disorganized, and the countertops were scattered with an array of toiletries, some bottles spilled over onto their sides. The wastebasket was surrounded by a pile of tissues, cast haphazardly onto the floor. In the bedroom, the drawers and closets were open, and clothes lay in tumbled clutters, some still on hangers from a dry cleaners, others dangling out of drawers. Shoes spilled out of the closet onto the floor. The bed was unmade, and the sheets were pulled off, as if Sommers had intended to change them. The mattress had slipped a little off-center from the box springs.

Outside, Branden helped Niell pack the lamp, pole, and battery into their carrying case in the back of Niell's 4x4. Then he thanked the deputy and said, "Something's not right, Ricky."

Niell rested his elbows on the side of the truck bed and said, "The house looks torn up."

Branden nodded. "Exactly."

Wilsher came out with his cameras and stowed the equipment in the trunk of his cruiser. At the back of Niell's truck, he said, "Sorry about Sommers, Mike. Nobody's been able to track her down."

"There's nothing more you can do?" Branden asked.

"Not unless we get another lead."

"You know about the kid who shot J. R. Weaver's horse?"

"You've got that nailed down?"

"Just last night. They weren't certain, but Larry Yoder's parents told me they think he was trying to tell them that he shot Weaver's horse."

"Where's Yoder now?" Wilsher asked.

"The psych ward at Aultman Hospital," Branden said.

"Now, that's just great."

"Maybe you could get a warrant for his home," Branden offered.

"With him in a hospital and only his parents' word? I doubt it."

"It wouldn't hurt to try."

"That much I'll do."

"Let me know what you find?"

"Better than that," Wilsher said. "I'll ask you to go on the search, when we get the warrant."

20

THE psychiatric ward at Canton's Aultman Hospital was located on the fourth floor. Branden stepped off the elevator and found himself in a small waiting room with several chairs, magazine racks on the wall, and a single floor lamp. The door to the psychiatric ward was made of polished aluminum with a small reinforced Plexiglas window. He tried the door and found it locked.

Beyond the door, he could see a nurses' station set back from a long corridor with doors to patients' rooms on either side. When he rang in at the intercom beside the door, a nurse poked her head out into the hall. She looked him over skeptically from her desk and sat back to use the intercom, saying only, "Yes?"

Branden considered the range of official and unofficial pretexts he could give and settled for, "I'd like to talk to Larry Yoder."

In a weary tone, the nurse said, "Mr. Yoder can't have any visitors."

Branden thought about a response for a moment, with his finger resting lightly over the intercom button. "I just need a few minutes," he said.

"Mr. Yoder is heavily sedated and can't have visitors."

"I've come from his family," Branden explained. "They're worried about him and have asked me to inquire."

"Even his family couldn't get in to see him now," the nurse said impatiently.

Branden's hand slipped to his front jeans pocket, and he felt the reserve deputy sheriff's badge there, wondering if a more official approach might open doors. He decided it wouldn't.

"Then can you come out to talk with me?" Branden asked. He watched the nurses' station and saw the nurse lean out over the counter and peer at him from behind the wall.

She studied him a moment and said, "I can't leave the ward. We're doing bed checks."

"If I were to wait?" Branden asked, face close to the speaker.

"It'd be a while," still leaning out over the counter.

"I'll wait," he said.

"Suit yourself, but like I said, it'll be a while, and you still can't see Mr. Yoder."

"When you can, I'd appreciate it," Branden said.

In the long hall behind the locked door, nurses and orderlies moved from room to room with clipboards. A nurse in a blue coat carried a tray of medicines in little white paper cups into the room nearest him.

He took a chair beside an end table piled with magazines. He waited there for nearly an hour and was idly turning the pages on his second issue of *Southern Living* when the nurse came out and repeated, "Mr. Yoder can't have visitors."

As he rose from the chair, Branden held out his hand and said, "I'm Dr. Michael Branden. From Millersburg. And I'm making a courtesy call on behalf of the family."

The nurse, a tall, slender woman dressed in a sagging white coat, pockets bulging with pens, paper, tissues, rubber gloves, and a stethoscope, said, "I'm sorry, Dr. Branden. You know how it works."

"Can you tell me anything about Mr. Yoder, then?" he asked.

"I can only say that his doctor has ordered no visitors. It'd be useless to try talking to Mr. Yoder, anyway, as heavily medicated as he is."

"Can you tell me when he might be able to have visitors?"

"I couldn't even guess when we'll take his restraints off," the nurse said and turned to key herself back onto the ward.

"Then can I speak with his doctor?" Branden asked.

"He's not here now," the nurse said, turning back to Branden with her hand on the latch.

"While he makes his rounds?" Branden suggested.

"Possibly," the nurse said, as she swiped her magnetic key through the lock box. "That's usually about 2:00 P.M."

Branden checked his watch, saw the nurse retreating down the hall, took the elevator to the ground floor, and bought coffee and a sandwich in the hospital's cafeteria. As he sat at one of the metal tables near a window, the insurance agent, Robert Cravely, approached Branden's table, introduced himself, and sat down on the other side, saying, "Professor Branden. Are you here to see Larry Yoder?"

Cravely was a weary-looking man, with a pudgy build and no remarkable features other than what appeared to be a permanent haphazard look about him. His plain gray suit was rumpled and worn nearly threadbare at the elbows. His unstylish, narrow blue tie was loosened at the neck. He set a battered briefcase on the table, snapped the worn metal latches open, and rummaged through an assortment of papers. He brought out a small notebook and an ornate fountain pen.

Branden said, "If you're here to see Larry Yoder, they're not letting anyone in."

"Tried earlier," Cravely said. "So you tried to see him, too?"

Branden nodded. "The nurses won't let me in. Why are you interested in Yoder?"

"The way I hear things," Cravely said, "you figure Yoder shot Weaver's horse."

Branden was surprised. "You seem to know a lot about the case," he said.

"I've got to," Cravely said. "Like I said Tuesday, I work for the insurance carrier for the furniture company whose truck jackknifed on 515 last Monday. We're not going to pay off with so many fatalities. Not until I understand all of the facts."

Branden argued, "Your driver dumped his rig on top of a car and a buggy, and caused the deaths of four people. I should think you'll be paying out a great deal of money before this is all over."

Cravely gave a snide laugh and said, "And I suppose it's a coincidence that you've got the coroner looking at a bullet they pulled out of the horse."

Branden withheld comment.

"And I suppose you don't think Larry Yoder, here, fired that shot," Cravely pushed.

"I'm paying a visit on behalf of the family," Branden said dryly.

"Right," Cravely said with practiced sarcasm.

Branden took a slow drink of coffee and wondered what Cravely would do once he learned that Brad Smith's parents had hired a P.I. out of Chicago. "Your driver had been drinking, and he came over that hill too fast. Yoder's shooting the horse, if he did in fact do that, has no bearing on what caused your truck to wreck."

Cravely put his notebook and pen back into the briefcase, closed the lid, pushed his chair back slowly, and stood up. With his wrist twisting the briefcase nervously at his side, Cravely said, "That was a new driver out there that day. The regular driver had taken sick. He normally makes two trips a week, year 'round, hauling Amish-made furniture to the stores in Chicago. But this new guy didn't know the roads, and I doubt any jury's going to blame my company for that crash, especially once it's clear what Larry Yoder did to Weaver's horse. He actually killed everybody out there, mind you, and our driver is to blame? I don't think so."

"Your man was drunk, Cravely."

"Under the legal limit."

"Not for a commercial driver."

Cravely frowned thinly.

Branden added, "And it's not at all certain that Larry Yoder killed any horse at all."

Cravely snorted skeptically, turned, and walked out. Branden finished his coffee and rode the elevators to the fourth floor. When he pushed the buzzer at the door to the psychiatric floor, another nurse answered him at the intercom.

"Dr. Michael Branden," the professor said. "To see Mr. Larry Yoder's psychiatrist."

The nurse replied, "One moment please," and the speaker fell silent. After about a minute, the nurse asked, "Do you have an appointment?"

"Not really," Branden said. "I'm from Millersburg, and I'm inquiring about Mr. Yoder as a courtesy to his family."

After another delay, the door to the psych unit buzzed, and Branden pushed the latch and walked onto the floor, toward the nurses' station. As he approached, a chubby doctor in a short white coat came out from behind the counter, stepped briskly toward Branden, held out his hand, and said, "Dr. Branden. I'm Dr. Waverly. Dr. Allan Waverly, The Third."

His handshake was gentle and his hand was soft, the consequence of a profession spent handling nothing harsher than paper and pens, perhaps keyboards. His cheeks were puffy and shaded a delicate rose. His fair skin contrasted pleasantly with his fine black hair. His eyes, though haggard, took in Branden with an intelligent sweep, the inspection of a man accustomed to forming opinions quickly.

Branden shook the doctor's hand and said, "Dr. Michael Branden, Ph.D."

"You're not medical?" Waverly asked, dismissively.

"Ph.D., Dr. Waverly. Civil War history."

Waverly turned to fiddle with one of the charts that were laid out on the nurses' counter. He took one of the clipboards, held it stiffly under his arm and said, "You'd never have gotten onto this floor if we'd known you weren't medical."

"I know," Branden said, and made an apologetic expression. "But I won't take a minute of your time, and I had hoped you could let me talk to Larry Yoder. Or that maybe you would talk to me about him."

"Civil War history?" Waverly asked, softening. "Where'd you take your degree?"

"Duke," Branden said.

"I'm Duke medical school!" Waverly exclaimed. His posture relaxed noticeably. "Class of '79."

"Seventy-three," Branden said. "You missed the big student sit-ins."

Dr. Waverly held the clipboard flat against his chest by crossing his arms over it, and he set his feet close together, back straight, in an aloof, professional stance, like a socialite at a cocktail party, trying to impress a rival classmate. "You were asking about Yoder?" he said.

"Right," Branden said. "Larry Yoder from Millersburg. His family brought him in Thursday."

"Brought him in with a pillowcase full of money," Waverly said. "Literally. Large denomination bills. Wanted to pay in advance."

"Not surprised," Branden said and then asked, "How is Yoder?"

"Come with me," Waverly said and walked slowly down the hall to a door at the far end, on the right. He held the heavy wooden door open for Branden and followed the professor into a large, bright room, where intense sunlight flooded in through reinforced Plexiglas. Branden stepped to the windows to orient himself and saw heat shimmers rising from the top level of the concrete parking tower to the south. His eyes focused closer, and on the windows he saw dozens of scratch marks in the safety glass. In one place, Branden read a ragged note saying, "Joseph was here—1979."

Close to the windows, Larry Yoder was strapped on his back into a tall hospital bed with railings, pillows arranged under his knees. Restraints made of heavy canvas were fastened to clamps under the bed, giving little freedom of movement for either Yoder's legs or his arms. The chart that hung at the foot of his bed was lettered "SUICIDAL" in red. An IV stand stood at the side of the bed, and several bags of solution fed a line that was taped to the back of Yoder's left hand, bruised and swollen where the needle punctured the skin.

A nurse came into the room and stood beside the chart at the foot of the bed, waiting to see if Waverly had any questions. Waverly asked, "Any change?" and the nurse said, "His legs are more restless at times." Waverly nodded, and she left.

Yoder lay perfectly still, with his eyes open. As Waverly and the professor stepped closer to his bed, Yoder's eyes turned in their direction briefly, and then turned slowly back to the ceiling.

"How are you feeling today?" Waverly asked, and rubbed lightly at the hairs on Yoder's arm.

Yoder gave the slightest tilt of his head, and tears flooded his eyes and ran down his temples. Waverly moved to the foot of the bed, pulled back the light blue blanket, and squeezed gently on Yoder's toes. He ran his thumbnail along the arch of Yoder's foot, and there was no movement. Waverly replaced the blanket and made an entry on his chart.

To Branden he said, "I doubt if Mr. Yoder will be able to tell us much today," and led Branden out into the hall. Waverly took his prim stance again, with his feet close together and his arms crossed over his chest, embracing the clipboard.

"Is that from his medications, or from his illness?" Branden asked.

"Most likely both," Waverly said. "But the medication would

be enough. First, he's on Depakote for the bipolar disorder. Then there's Ativan and Desyrel, all at the maximum dose. I wrote orders this morning for Risperdal, too—he may be somewhat psychotic right now. So I'm not expecting him to have much to say for a while. You should tell his family that it'll take some time before we can start any psychotherapy. It might be a week or more before he even makes it out of his room for Group. Even crafts are doubtful at this juncture. Once we get him stabilized, I'll back down the Ativan, and he won't sleep so much. Could be a week or two."

Branden thought about the Yoder family and about John Weaver and Britta Sommers. He looked at Yoder in his bed, frail with desperate eyes, and he remembered the burning cars at the crash scene and the twisted buggy parts scattered over thirty yards of road and field. He thought of the heavy smoke odor inside Sommers's ranch house, and he remembered the expressions on the faces of eight Amish men who had received letters from John R. Weaver. He asked, "Did he say anything when they brought him in?"

"Not Larry," Waverly said. "His mother told me he shot a horse." He waited with a coaxing expression for an explanation.

Branden offered nothing, and Waverly added, dubiously, "She told me he shot a horse and killed several people. Sounds a bit extreme for your neck of the woods, but if that were true, I'd need to know it."

Branden looked back into Yoder's room and studied the small, pathetic form that was laid out in the bed. He turned slowly back into the hall, letting the door close softly. He faced Waverly and said, "I think he probably did, Dr. Waverly. Shoot a horse, that is."

21

Saturday, August 12
4:45 P.M.

AT AKRON Children's Hospital, Branden parked in the out-
door lot on Bowery Street. He climbed one flight of stairs to the
skyway over Bowery, and entered the hospital near the main reception counter. On the right-hand wall in the corridor outside
the burn unit, he saw a display of fifty or so fire department arm
patches, and opposite that, the outside counter for the unit. He
asked about Robertson and was told to lift the receiver on a
phone at the end of the hall. At the phone, he explained the na-
ture of his visit, and a nurse from inside the burn unit emerged
and instructed him to wash his hands and put on a bright yellow paper gown and mask, each of which fastened in back with
tape strips.

Inside the burn unit, Branden found Melissa Taggert in a
white doctor's coat, standing next to the central station outside
Robertson's room.

Branden walked directly to her and asked, "What's his con-
dition, Missy?"

"It's worse than I originally thought," she said, eyes weary
and bloodshot. "They've run some cultures and found out he
has a yeast infection. Which means they've switched him to
amphotericin. Then last night he grew confused. Became restless.
His temperature dropped, and so did his blood pressure. Also
tachycardia, which means he's getting worse. Some vital organs

might become involved, if the infection takes hold. Any way you figure it, Mike, he's worse. Much worse than we realized."

Inside Robertson's room, Branden found the big sheriff on a large air bed, with three IV poles holding five IV pumps on the left side, at the sheriff's head. Several monitors crowded on stands on the right of his bed. Robertson lay on his back. The edges of white thermazine and gauze bandages showed under his back and arms. The tube from a Foley catheter ran out between his legs, and there was a CVP line in his chest, with four ports. An arterial line ran from his arm to a blood pressure monitor. Branden read the labels on several of the bags that were piped to the central line and saw morphine, lactated Ringers, and ativan. The blinking monitors and pumps kept up a steady chorus of low beeps and clicks in what was otherwise a dim and silent room.

Branden took Bruce Robertson's big hand and gave a gentle squeeze. Missy Taggert watched from the foot of the bed as Branden pulled a chair closer with the point of his foot. He sat down still holding to Robertson's hand, and said, "Bruce, it's Mike."

There was no response, and Taggert's eyes dropped. She nodded sadly to the professor and turned slowly to leave the room. Branden saw in her expression the same sorrow and helpless despair that he had seen in Caroline's eyes after her miscarriages. Limitless grief, mixed bravely with determined self-control.

He spoke again to Robertson, again without a response. With the sheriff's large hand cradled in both of his, the professor leaned over beside the bed, thinking. Also praying.

In time, Robertson stirred in his bed, lifted his head weakly, and gave the professor's hand a squeeze. He said, "Hey, Mike," with effort, and lay back on the pillow. "If you don't let go of my hand, people gonna think we're dating."

Branden gently eased his hand away and said, "Looks like you've pretty well done it this time, Sheriff."

Robertson's eyes spoke of pain and exhaustion. Tears formed in them, and he tried to raise a hand to dry them. He failed in the task, and, as a line of tears streamed down his cheeks, the sheriff said, "They keep putting drops in my eyes."

"I'll tell them to stop," Branden said, and cleared his throat with difficulty.

Robertson rolled his head slowly from side to side and closed his eyes. When he opened them again, he whispered, "Still there, Mike?"

"Still here," Branden said, and, "You need to rest."

"Seems like I need to pay more attention to Missy Taggert."

"She spoke to you?"

Robertson nodded weakly.

"She told me she was going to do that, before they flew you up here."

"Got my first ride in a chopper and can't remember a thing," Robertson complained, and fell silent. When he spoke again, it was in a softer voice. "Seems I need to let Renie Cotton go."

"It's time, Bruce. Renie's been gone a long time, now. If you can do it, Taggert's a fine woman."

"I've always liked her," Robertson said quietly. "A lot."

"I know."

"You knew."

"I knew. I wouldn't say it was obvious, but I knew."

"Great. Now I suppose you're gonna tell me Missy knows, too."

"I think she does, Bruce."

"I always thought Renie would be the only one."

"Kinda gives you something to look forward to."

"Don't kid a kidder, Mike."

Branden didn't respond.

Robertson squeezed his eyes shut and said, "It's obvious, Professor. She wouldn't have told me anything of the sort, if she thought I was for sure gonna make it."

"Stop being a knucklehead, Bruce."

"A knucklehead."

"Right. You're a giant knucklehead, and you're gonna pull through just fine."

Robertson smiled.

22

CAL Troyer and Bishop Andy Weaver sat in the afternoon heat on the deacon's bench on the bishop's front porch, pondering the troubles J. R. Weaver had dropped into the laps of eight district families before he died. They had been sitting there since the big meal the women had served following church services. Several men stood on the porch, listening, sometimes commenting. Others sat in small groups on chairs in the shade under trees. There were three men on hay bales beside the barn, where the roof overhang provided some shade. Among the older men, a few had lit pipes, and several of the younger men smoked cigarettes. A gang of young boys scampered out of one red barn and into another, shouting boisterously in their game of tag. A small group of girls, perhaps nine or ten years old, stood nearby, laughing, taunting, and making open sport of the boys. Older boys stood here and there, vests undone, talking with men, mostly about farming. One couple, a boy and a girl about sixteen, tried to slip unnoticed behind the house and were immediately set upon by younger children, teasing them mercilessly. A woman wearing a white apron over a dark plum dress came out onto the front porch drying her hands on a kitchen towel. She spoke briefly to the bishop and took his coffee mug back into the house. An elder and his wife waved from their buggy beside the fence and then climbed in and started slowly down the gravel drive, headed home.

Cal was saying, "I don't know what to tell you, Andy. It could be anybody's kids mixed in with this."

"It's hard to imagine there are youngsters like that around here," Andy said morosely.

"They're probably not Amish."

"I have to assume that two of them are Amish. Or at least that they could be. The people have been asking."

Andy took a toothpick from his shirt pocket and began working it silently between two front teeth. He thought for a while and added, "They are common thieves, nothing better. Robbers, but the masks make it so much worse than folk realize."

"It's not your fault," Cal said.

"It falls under my authority," Andy said. "You know the *Ordnung*."

Cal nodded his understanding. The *Ordnung* spelled it all out. Even bishops had little choice, it seemed. "How many buggy robberies have there really been?"

"I know of nine, starting with John R. Weaver."

Cal whistled. "Does the sheriff know about all of those?"

"No, only four."

"You should tell the professor," Cal said and pointed to the small truck coming down the lane. Weaver put his finger to his lips to tell Cal to keep silent about the boys.

Branden drove slowly up to the house, raising as little dust as he could. He stopped a dozen-odd yards from the house to let the dust settle and climbed out of his air-conditioned cab into bright afternoon sun.

As he climbed the porch steps, the men who had gathered around to listen to Cal and the bishop departed quietly, some into the house, some onto the lawn. Branden pulled a wooden chair up backwards in front of Cal and Andy and sat down, legs straddling the seat, arms resting on the back.

Cal said, "Do you know, Mike, how many buggy robberies the sheriff knows about?"

"Four, maybe five," Branden said. To Andy, he asked, "Have there been many in your district?"

"Can't be sure," Andy said, holding his toothpick between his teeth. "They've been mostly to the north, up around Winesburg."

"They dress Amish, but I doubt they actually are," Branden said.

"Small comfort," Andy said flatly and eyed Cal sideways.

After a quiet interlude, the bishop remarked, "Larry Yoder's parents should not have been seeing him, much less taking meals with him. That only encourages a person to continue a sinful lifestyle. But those are just the rules, the *Ordnung*. Eventually, I've got to get the people back into the scriptures. That's the real crisis of leadership. Getting at the scriptures on which the *Ordnung* is based."

"Few bishops bother anymore," Cal said.

"I'm trying for something better, Cal. But there's a more immediate problem, Professor. Cal and I have been wondering what to do about our eight families. Dozers and dump trucks are going to show up at one of those farms one day, and then we'll have to know what to do."

"How many options do you really have?" Branden asked.

Weaver asked, "Have you had a chance to talk to that lawyer?"

"I'll try tomorrow. After my appointment at the bank."

Weaver sighed, looking resigned to the worst. "Jobs in town are out of the question," he said.

"Is there nothing else?" Cal asked.

"You could fight the eviction in court. Get an injunction," Branden said.

Weaver shook his head. "We've got a collection started among the families of the district to see if we can buy land hereabouts for the men to farm."

"Is there that much land for sale?" Cal asked.

Weaver leaned over on his elbows and shook his head again, eyes cast down at his feet. "Can you drive me up to Cleveland, tomorrow, Cal?"

Cal answered, "Yes," with hesitation.

Weaver stared at his Sunday brogans for a moment and said, "I've sent out a dozen or so letters to settlements in other states."

Cal shifted forward on the bench. "Moving?" he asked.

"Maybe Holmes County is no good for us anymore," Weaver said. "Land values too high. Too much development."

"That's a lot of people to move," Cal said.

"I have to preserve the old ways, Cal."

"What about a good old-fashioned protest?" Cal offered.

Weaver seemed puzzled.

"You know. A sit-in. Lie down in front of the dozers. Something like that."

"Resist the developers?" Weaver asked.

"Yes," Branden said. "Make it difficult for them to develop the land."

"If we did that, there would be a confrontation," Weaver said. "That's not the Amish way. It violates the *Ordnung*. If people are bent on harming us, we avoid them. No, I am still figuring you can get something from your lawyer."

"What are you going to do in the meantime?" Cal asked.

"Only one thing we can do, Cal. You and I are going to pay a visit tomorrow to the offices of Holmes Estates."

"I thought you didn't want a confrontation," Cal said.

"There is nothing in the *Ordnung* that forbids good horse trading," Weaver answered wryly.

23

Monday, August 14
9:55 A.M.

BRANDEN arrived five minutes early for his appointment with the new trustee of J. R. Weaver's estate and sat in the second-floor hallway of the bank, two doors down from Britta Sommers's empty office. At precisely 10:00 A.M., the secretary lifted the phone, announced the professor, listened briefly, and then escorted Branden into Ted Brownell's small room. Brownell appeared young, maybe thirty-five, and sat in a worn gray suit behind a desk cluttered with loose papers and colored file folders.

Branden stepped forward, offered his hand, and said, "Ted, it's been a long time. How are you doing?"

"Nice to see you again, Professor," Brownell said formally.

"You graduated maybe fifteen years ago, Ted. I think it's about time you called me Mike."

Brownell shifted uneasily on his feet and said, "Oh, I could never do that, Professor."

"What was my nickname then?"

"Sir?"

"I get a new nickname from the history majors every few years. What was it when you came through?"

"I don't know, Professor."

"Sure you do, Ted. These days it's Doc. I'm sure you must

have had one too. About that time it was Getty, I think. Because I started teaching that course on Gettysburg."

Brownell's cheeks flushed a bright rose, as did the tops of his ears. He said, "I don't know, Professor," but was altogether unable to mask the smile that formed on his lips.

Branden eyed him mischievously for a few seconds, laughed, and said, "Anyway, please call me Mike."

"OK, Professor."

Branden took a seat at the side of Brownell's desk and laid his right forearm along the top edge of the desk. Leaning forward casually, he said, "I understand Britta Sommers transferred John Weaver's trust to you."

Brownell stretched his arms out to indicate all of the papers and folders on the desktop. "I've only now started going through the thing. Sommers was very thorough, it seems, and meticulous."

"What all have you got there, Ted?" Branden asked.

"It looks like the usual records. Stocks, bonds, and mutual funds. Papers of incorporation. Partnerships. A will. Some very current listings of his land holdings, including a recent sale—quite large, really—and estimates of net worth over the years. That sort of thing."

"What's in the will, Ted?"

"I can't tell you that, Professor. It hasn't all been executed, yet. Weaver's lawyer is working through it, and I'm supposed to get the figures to him this week."

"Do you think his lawyer could tell me about the will? What's his name?"

"Henry DiSalvo, and I doubt it. There's a provision that makes the will public only after a certain period of time has elapsed."

"I know DiSalvo," Branden said, casually. "How much time before he announces the will?"

"Professor, I really can't say."

Branden noticed an uneasiness in Brownell's voice and changed the subject, trying a different tack. "You went to grad school, didn't you, Ted?"

"I took an M.B.A. at Miami University. Then Capital University Law School."

"You've done well."

"I should have practiced law, Professor. Banks don't pay very much," Brownell said, fingering the lapel on his well-worn suit.

Branden let a moment pass, and then Brownell said, "You know, I saw Weaver the day he died."

"I didn't know that."

"Yes. He was here to go over some new papers that morning. His last land sale. He and his lawyer had all the work done, and Weaver wanted copies of all the deeds and papers put into his file, here. He did everything that way, it seems, and now I've got a desk full of documents to go through."

"Any idea how much he was worth?" Branden asked, nonchalantly.

"Couldn't say. Wouldn't be able to tell you anyway. It's all going to come out when his will is read."

"At the right time?" Branden said.

"And with the right people present," Brownell answered. "Look, Professor. If you want to get the details on the last big sell-off, they'll have it all down at the map office. Or it might have gotten to the auditor by now. The recorder will have it in a few days at the most, and it'll be public record, then. Probably is now, anyway."

"Oh, I can wait, Ted. I was just hoping you could give me some of the details."

Brownell gave an apologetic shrug of his shoulders.

"Maybe Britta Sommers's end of it, then?" Branden asked.

"What do you mean?"

"Like how much Sommers had mixed in with Weaver's business."

"She shouldn't have any," Brownell said and sat up straighter. His eyes focused more sharply on Branden.

Branden remembered the notations on the numerous files Weaver had kept at his home, indicating a small percentage had gone to Sommers from many of his deals. Discreetly, he said, "Nothing with Sommers?"

Sternly, Brownell said, "It's bank policy. Trust officers are not to involve themselves in the business affairs of their clients. She could have lost her job."

Branden said, "I don't suppose she has come in recently?"

"We don't expect her. Tuesday last week was her last day on the job."

Outside, Branden walked north on Clay Street. He was troubled by the revelation that Britta Sommers had rounded off the crisp edges of professional ethics, according to Brownell. He cut across the lawn in front of the courthouse and took Monroe to the county recorder's offices. Distracted, he barely greeted the two ladies at the front counter. At the computer terminal in the back of the room, he punched mechanically on the keyboard and immediately found a string of entries recording land transactions between Holmes Estates, and Weaver and Sommers. The numbers added up in his mind with a strange sedating effect, so that eventually the millions seemed like trivial sums to him. So that the magnitude of the land sales no longer astonished him. And he realized that there might very well be a good reason why Britta Sommers would leave town so suddenly.

24

Monday, August 14
11:30 A.M.

HENRY DiSalvo's one-room law office was on the second floor of an old downtown building. The only indication of its location was faded brown lettering on a narrow, street-level door. Branden pushed through the door and climbed the staircase to the second floor. He knocked on the door at the top of the steps and walked into the office. DiSalvo sat with his back to the door, typing steadily on the keys of an outmoded computer. He turned around, saw the professor, and rose to shake hands.

"Mike," DiSalvo said. "Good to see you."

"Henry," Branden said, and glanced around the old-fashioned office, little changed from the days when DiSalvo had managed young Branden's finances after his parents' fatal car crash.

DiSalvo himself had aged markedly in recent years, Branden noted, and what hair remained was white. His tattered suit hinted of an impoverished state, though in fact he was one of the wealthiest men in Millersburg. His office was spartan in appointments, cluttered everywhere with papers, folders, and briefs. An odd assortment of gray metal desks, in a style popular in the fifties, stood along the walls. The floor was of dark wood, the finish worn through in patches. There were no rugs or carpeting, and dust bunnies had gathered in the corners and under furniture. The frames of the photos, plaques, and diplomas were dusty on the top edges, and some hung crooked on the wall. A small window air conditioner rattled and hummed near the floor, at the bottom of one of the tall, street-side windows. Most of the drapes were pulled closed against the sun, and with only the desk lamp burning next to DiSalvo's computer, dusk seemed to have fallen in the room.

DiSalvo came around his desk, moved a stack of papers and books from a chair in front, and offered Branden a seat. As he walked to the other side of his desk and sat down, he asked, "Is your parents' trust still producing for you?"

"Very well, Henry. You did an excellent job."

"A tragedy, how your parents died," DiSalvo reflected. "I hope the money has been a help to you over the years."

"It was a great help at first, in graduate school and later. Now, I let it accumulate and pay a secretary out of the proceeds."

"Secretaries!" DiSalvo exclaimed. "By the time I explain to them what I want, I could have done it myself."

"I've got a good one, Henry, and I suspect you could find one, too," Branden said gently, smiling.

DiSalvo smiled back and then laughed outright. "Not at my age," he said. "But I doubt you came here to harass me about my personality."

"I need to talk to you about J. R. Weaver's will. His recent land deals, too."

"You're mixed up in that?" DiSalvo asked.

"Helping the sheriff."

"How is he?"

"Not good. Still at the Akron burn unit. I'm going up there again tonight."

"Let me know," DiSalvo said. "As far as Weaver goes, I really can't discuss it now. How about Wednesday morning?" DiSalvo turned the pages of his desk calendar and held a pen ready to ink in an appointment.

Branden said, "Fine. Eleven A.M. suits me."

DiSalvo wrote on his calendar and nodded.

Branden rose and said, "Can you tell me anything about his will?"

"Not really," DiSalvo said, seated. "It can't be disclosed as yet."

"Why?"

"A certain provision says I'm to hold it until specific conditions have been met. I can't file it until then."

"Rather strange," Branden commented.

"Oh, it won't be long, Mike. Just a few more days."

Branden said, "I'll see you Wednesday," and moved toward the door. With his hand on the knob, he turned back to DiSalvo and asked, "Do you know anything about Britta Sommers's business dealings with Weaver?"

"No," DiSalvo said. "And if I did, I wouldn't tell anyone."

"Why not?"

"She served as his trustee. There'd be ethical problems."

"She's missing, Henry. You know her house was torched last Thursday."

DiSalvo nodded, frowned, and rubbed nervously at the back of his head. "She did sell some land in Weaver's last deal. A parallel transaction. Nothing that could be construed as improper."

"Is that land deal final?"

"All the ink is dry, if that's what you mean. The papers have been filed."

"Any chance of reversing the deal?"

"No."

Branden thanked him and let himself out. Once down to the street, he decided to visit Bobby Newell and walked the three hot and noisy blocks to the jail. Ellie Troyer sent him through to the sheriff's office, and Branden found the captain in uniform, standing with a large mug of coffee at one of the tall office windows facing the square.

Newell turned from the window, and before Branden could say anything, barked, "Arden Dobrowski has filed charges against you, Professor."

Branden laughed and said, "What charges?"

"Says you hit him."

"The man deserved it, Bobby," Branden scoffed.

"Wouldn't surprise me, but he's filed charges."

"Is he pressing those charges?"

"Not at the moment, but he's coming in this afternoon to talk about it, and you had best be hoping I'll be able to talk him down."

"Can't be bothered," Branden said and sat casually in a chair next to Robertson's cherry desk.

Newell parked his muscular frame on the corner of the desk near Branden and said, "I think you ought to back out of the Weaver/Sommers case for a while. She's still missing. We've tried to find her, but she's left town or something."

"That doesn't mean she's mixed up in the Weaver murder," Branden said.

"With her house burnt up?"

"If anybody is mixed up in the Weaver murder, it's Larry Yoder. Have you got a warrant to search his place yet?"

"All we have is your word that his parents said something about what Yoder might have said, drunk a few days ago."

"Talk to his parents yourself."

"Yoder's father has not been cooperative."

"It's his mother who will talk," Branden said. "What about his psychiatrist? I tried him once, with no luck. Maybe you could get something out of him."

"He probably won't tell us a thing either."

"Yoder's not going to be in the hospital forever," said Branden. "What have you done about him?"

"Wilsher sent Armbruster up there yesterday with a letter announcing our official intent to arrest Yoder once he is discharged from the hospital."

"You think they'll honor that?"

"They usually do. I've asked for a confirming letter of reply."

"Any other leads?"

"Yes," Newell said, and stopped.

"Well?" Branden pressed.

"I want you to take a breather, Mike. Walk a buggy over north of Walnut Creek, until we sort this out."

"You think we've still got a chance at those kids?"

"It's possible. Anyways, I want you to take the rest of today. Let me cool off Dobrowski and follow up some leads."

"What leads?"

"You're in a buggy this afternoon, right?"

"OK. What leads?"

"It was a 30-06."

"Seems plausible. But how is that a lead?"

"That bullet you had Missy Taggert pull out of Weaver's buggy horse? Well, Professor, there is a photo on Weaver's wall. Weaver, Yoder, and Jim Weston out West with the elk they shot. We're talking to Weston now, and it turns out the three of them used to drive a van out to Colorado each year and hunt. Weston was the driver, and Yoder was something like a hired hand."

"So?"

"So, it looks like we might just get that warrant, after all. In the picture under the elk, Larry Yoder is holding what Weston says is a 30-06. One of Weaver's rifles, and it's not on the rack in Weaver's study."

25

Monday, August 14
4:15 P.M.

IT TOOK the professor the better part of the afternoon to suit up in Amish costume, collect his camera, gear, and revolver, borrow a horse and buggy from the Hershbergers, and start walking the rig along Township Lane T-414. The temperature had climbed to ninety-six degrees, skies were clear, and the sun was as bright as in the painted desert.

Giving the horse rein to set its own pace, Branden slouched against the right side of the buggy, with his arms crossed over his chest, seeming to nap. With his weight off-center, the rig leaned heavily to the right, and, more often than not, he was three-wheeling, the left rear wheel raised off the pavement.

Satisfied that he would appear vulnerable to teenage bandits, he traveled the gravel lanes of Walnut Creek Township peacefully for about an hour, mulling over the Weaver/Yoder case.

On one stretch of lane, a girl in a pink dress and white prayer cap passed on a mountain bike, blue plastic grocery bags hanging from the handlebars. A blacksmith shop came up on the right, set close to the lane. Behind, there was an aluminum-sided, white split-level house, with laundry hanging on lines at the side, and a long run of fence made of wide brown boards, separating house from pasture.

A little farther along, he pulled back on the reins, stopped the horse under the shade of a spreading maple, climbed out of the buggy while still holding the reins, and rubbed the heel of his left hand hard against the small of his back. Then he arched backward and rolled his slender torso left and right. Up straight again, he rubbed at his back with his right hand, and then he leaned forward and slowly reached for his toes, first on one side and then on the other. When he straightened up, he walked in front of the horse and tied the reins to a fence post overgrown with tall, dried weeds and grasses. Next to the fence post, the trunk of the maple had grown outward to encase the rusted barbed wires, pushing the ancient fence out several feet toward the road.

Branden reached in to the floor of the buggy and pulled out a narrow plastic bottle of water. As soon as he had finished that one, he started on another. He had brought five for the trip and now wished it had been a dozen. He stepped clear of the buggy, slapped his straw hat against his shins to knock the dust off his pants, and then laid the light-cream hat back softly on his head. As he stood enjoying the shade, he studied the lane, first in one direction and then in the other, and at last untied the reins, climbed back in, and headed off at the same slow pace.

As he rode along peacefully, deep in thought, he barely registered the monotonous crunch of the buggy wheels on gravel and the horse's slow, deliberate footfalls. The dust and the sun gave a hot, dry, stinging quality to the air. From time to time he would linger under an overhanging tree, where the shade cut the glare and the heat.

A young boy came shuffling along barefoot in the gravel, dressed in blue denim trousers with denim suspenders, a blue cotton shirt with the collar open, and a cream straw hat with the top broken out. The next farm along the lane had cinder-block silos with silver metal domes. Two girls were turning into the drive, pulling a wagon that held several bags of groceries and their sleepy younger brother. The girls were both attired in rose dresses, laced white aprons, and black bonnets.

As Branden started a left turn into the Shetlers' driveway to water the horse, a car horn sounded behind him. He pulled himself across the seat and looked around the side curtains of the buggy to see Ricky Niell parking a cruiser in the shade of the berm. Branden pulled back on the reins and set the hand brake. He stayed on the buggy's seat, and Niell strolled up to the left side. As he wiped the inside of his hatband with a handkerchief, Niell asked, "Hot enough for you?"

Branden laughed and handed Niell one of his water bottles.

"Thanks," Niell said, and set his black and gray summer hat back on his head. He unscrewed the lid, and after several big swallows, Niell said, "That camera's not going to do you any good, Professor."

"I had planned on waiting until they were off a ways, and then using the zoom lens."

"All you'll get is their backs," Niell said, "or their masks. Anyway, it's too dangerous for you to ride decoy anymore."

"How so?"

"I need to show you, Professor," Niell said. "You think you can get that rig back up a hollow? Dirt road most of the way."

"I can try."

"Maybe you'd better leave it here, and I'll take you," Niell said.

Branden walked the buggy into the drive, asked permission at the house to leave the horse tied up there, and fetched his revolver before getting into the cruiser with Niell and driving off.

After several turns onto narrow country lanes, Niell pulled up a rise on a weedy track into the woods. He crested a hill beside an overgrown fence line and followed the track through the timber into a little valley, heavily wooded, with large boulders protruding from the floor of the forest. The trail crossed a small stream bed, climbed steeply, and took a sharp turn left before leveling out onto a straight path into the back of the hollow. Niell slowed to a crawl, hit the top lights and siren, and pulled forward cautiously, saying, "I don't want to surprise anyone out here."

After a quarter of a mile, Niell pulled the cruiser over beside a small shed made of dilapidated boards with a flat, rusty tin roof. Niell shut off the engine and nervously tapped the steering wheel. "I'd like to know what you make of this," he said to Branden.

Branden and Niell got out and took a walk around the outside of the shed. The walls were covered with graffiti in red and black spray paint. One section of wall displayed a goat's head inside a pentagram, with "Satan Rules" in bold letters underneath. Other places had what appeared to be the lyrics of twisted songs, heavy metal, Branden thought. One inscription read, "Evil I love." Another, "God died with Satan."

Returning to the front, Branden pushed in on a swinging door and found the inside to be similarly painted with drawings of grotesque animals, heads mostly, with horns. The back wall was carefully decorated in red spray paint with a horned monster, full frame, with claws and gnarled legs.

The floor was a mixture of dried earth and cinders, and in the middle, a large circle surrounded a triangle, etched into the dirt with lime. In one corner of the triangle, a large post was set firmly into the ground. In a far corner, a mountain bike was propped against a wall, and a goat's-head mask hung from the padded seat.

Niell stepped outside first, obviously on edge.

Branden soon followed and asked, "How did you find it, Ricky?"

"A kind of triangulation," Niell said. "I interviewed all of the families who had been robbed in their buggies. Asked which way the robbers came from. Which way they rode off. Whether they made any turns into lanes the folks could see. Then I drew it all up on a map and boxed in an area where they always seemed to come from, or go to. It took another day and a half, but I finally came up this trail and found the thing."

"We've got something more than misguided teenaged robbers on our hands," Branden said.

"I know," Ricky said. "I've got to turn it all over to the captain. This place gives me the creeps."

As Niell drove back to the house where Branden's buggy was parked, neither spoke. When they got out of the cruiser, Niell, in a foul mood, brushed dust off his uniform with a frown. He asked, "You got the Weaver case all figured yet?"

"Not everything, Ricky," Branden said and sat again on the buggy's squeaky seat boards. "Some things don't fit at all. Bits and pieces, maybe, but not all of it."

"Yoder must have shot at Weaver," Niell said.

"True," Branden said. "But until he decides to talk, if he ever does, there's no way to tell whether he aimed at Weaver or at the horse."

"Or at the buggy," Niell said. "You know. Trying to intimidate Weaver into stopping the land sales."

"He had to know the land sales had all been finalized," Branden countered.

"All that does is change the motive."

"Revenge?" Branden said. He remembered the psych ward, and Yoder's small frame strapped into his bed, tears welling up and spilling over from his troubled eyes. Pathetic. Knocked over the edge by the death of a horse, from what his parents said. Depression. A suicide watch. "Yoder doesn't seem the type. We've probably got to consider the horse accidental."

"OK," Ricky said, "but you still can't tell if he wanted old man Weaver dead."

"Yoder's manic-depressive. Bipolar at the very least. Psychotic, too, according to his doctor."

Niell shook his head. "Maybe he just wanted to scare Weaver, and with his bad luck, he hit the horse."

"Now we've got the Satanic angle," Branden added.

"You think maybe the two are connected?"

"Can't say. I'd be more inclined to think Weaver's death is somehow connected with the fire at Sommers's house."

"Maybe those kids came back to finish their work," Niell said. "They once tried to rob him, you know."

Branden nodded, but added, "Then Sommers is worse than just missing."

"She could have set fire to her own house," Niell said.

"Why?"

"To throw suspicion off her. For the insurance money. Maybe to destroy evidence of her dealings with Weaver."

"But she knows we've got all of Weaver's files," Branden countered.

"Then where has she gone, Professor?"

Branden had no answer. "They tell me she shouldn't have had any business dealings with Weaver at all."

"Then that's her motive for disappearing," Niell said.

"She did say she had most of her affairs in order. Had her 'walking away' money in hand."

"We're never going to see her again," Niell asserted.

Branden's cell phone rang, and as he answered it, Niell returned to his car and made a radio report.

Back at the buggy, Niell said, "Ellie says the lieutenant wants me out at Yoder's house trailer. Jimmy Weston gave them enough for a warrant to search the premises."

Branden stared absently at his cell phone and quietly said, "Looks like you were wrong about Sommers, Ricky. We're going to see her after all. That was Dan Wilsher. They've found her in the trunk of Yoder's car."

26

Monday, August 14
4:50 P.M.

STUNNED into silence, Branden mechanically turned the horse. Niell drove off toward Yoder's home, and Branden returned the buggy to its owners. Once the horse was put up, he stowed his belongings in his trunk, and drove to 515, headed south toward Walnut Creek. He turned west onto 406, which meanders the rocky hillsides along the north edge of the Goose Bottoms. The narrow road turned and rose, dropped and doubled back, following Goose Creek. After two miles or so, he climbed a steep gravel drive into the woods beside the road. The drive curved sharply and came out into a hilltop clearing, where Branden pulled right to let an ambulance pass slowly by, on its way down the hill. When he pulled ahead, he found a brown and blue single-wide mobile home on foundation blocks. There was a rusty metal shed at the left end of the trailer and a carport with a green plastic roof on the right. A small sedan was parked under the carport, its trunk open. A deputy was feathering a dust brush along the front edge of the lid, looking for prints.

Branden stopped on the drive, some ways back from the trailer, and left the engine running. The ambulance had no need to hurry, he realized. The trunk ahead would be empty. Britta was gone.

Somehow, he had known it, at least on a certain level, all along. It had been foolish to have hoped otherwise. He had known it since his inspection with Niell of the rest of Britta's house. Too much clutter there for a woman who had kept so immaculate an office. And had there ever been a good reason to believe she had burned her own house? At best, he had hoped she was hiding for some reason.

He felt blunted and disoriented, unable to think. He drummed his thumbs compulsively on the steering wheel and fought an impulse to turn his car around and drive home. Her death left him feeling cheated and empty, like when photos of the recently deceased appear at ten-year reunions.

Slowly, Branden pulled in at an angle beside Niell's cruiser, in front of the trailer. As he climbed out into the heat, Dan Wilsher appeared in the doorway and waved him inside. Wilsher's uniform was damp with sweat under his arms and on his chest and back.

Inside, the short length of the trailer to the right of the door held a kitchen and a round kitchen table with a pink Formica top. Three metal chairs, with seat pads to match the color of the Formica, were pushed up under the table. At the table, Lieutenant Wilsher returned to his task, using forceps to drop long rifle cartridges into an evidence bag.

"These are 30-06 rounds, Mike," Wilsher said. "We found them scattered on the table and some down on the floor. We also found J. R. Weaver's missing 30-06 rifle out back behind some garbage cans. I sent it in for prints and to test-fire a cartridge."

"It's going to match the one Missy found in Weaver's horse," Branden asserted without satisfaction.

"No doubt," Wilsher said. He waved Deputy Armbruster over to finish bagging the cartridges, and he pulled Branden aside, to a small printer on a stand next to a computer table in the living area that adjoined the kitchen. He used his pen to lift the corner of a sheet of paper in the printer's out-tray. Branden bent low to read the text on the underside and found it to be a letter addressed to J. R. Weaver. The first lines read: "I'm not going to warn you again. Stop the foreclosures."

Wilsher called Ricky Niell over and said, "Bag this and then see if you can find any other files or letters like this, on the hard drive or on any of these other disks."

In the living area behind them, Wilsher pointed out a stack of brown paper grocery bags next to a faded, brown-and-red-checked sofa. Branden looked the room over and saw other bags cut open to lie flat, as rectangles. Several of these were spread out on a long, marred, wooden coffee table, and more had been wadded into large brown balls and tossed into a corner next to an easy chair with fabric to match the sofa. A box of children's crayons had been dropped on the worn, gray carpet, and Branden knelt to pick it up. Inside were the nibs and stubs of broken black, blue, and brown crayons. The other colors were missing.

While kneeling, Branden began studying the crayon drawings on the brown paper sheets arranged on the coffee table. On each heavy sheet, he found more or less the same sketch. There would be either a rectangle or a square, drawn in black crayon. Black or brown strokes carved the outer shape into sections with lines that had been pressed hard onto the paper, sometimes breaking a crayon and leaving a splotch or a veering line on the page. In what seemed to be a separate group of papers, the boxes and their dividing lines were carefully drafted. In others, which seemed to have been drawn with greater force, the dividing lines were more like slashes of crayon repeated over and over again, line after line, giving thick swatches of brown or black from crayons that had been flattened or broken, the anger in the crude drawings evident from the force that had been employed.

Wilsher watched Branden sort through the brown paper canvases and then retrieved two of the wadded balls of paper from the corner. He sat in the easy chair and unfolded one on his lap. The edges of the paper had been torn, not cut with scissors. The powerful strokes with crayon were more brutal than the ones Branden had found, but there was still the same rectangle, cut into sections by the flat stub of a crayon in an angry hand.

"There's a lot of rage in these drawings," Branden said.

"Out of control is what I'd call it," Wilsher said. He stood and started toward the hall leading to the back of the trailer. "I'd like you to see the bedroom, Mike," he said.

They found an unkempt room with empty whiskey bottles strewn here and there. The bed was unmade, and its sheets and covers were stuffed into a corner beside the headboard. Dirty dishes and the remains of several take-out meals lay on the stained mattress. A small television rested on a stand in a corner at the foot of the bed. It was an old black-and-white set, with a rotary dial for thirteen channels, plus UHF. The wire antenna was draped with crumpled sheets of aluminum foil. Branden used his handkerchief to turn the set on and got a hazy picture of an evangelist, Brother Dave from Canton, making a vigorous point about the scriptures that lay open in his hand.

Branden pushed the button off and helped Wilsher open the drawers on the two dressers in the room. They held an eclectic assortment of summer and winter clothes, and in one drawer there was also a stack of hunting photos, strapped together with a rubber band. Wilsher, wearing gloves now, removed the rubber band and starting leafing through the stack of photos. "Weaver, Weston, and Yoder, hunting out West," he said and laid the photos on top of the dresser.

Branden studied the photographs. One seemed to duplicate the photo that Newell had described to him, hanging on a wall in J. R. Weaver's study. Yoder, holding the 30-06 rifle beside an enormous elk. Wilsher gathered the photos together and dropped the lot into an evidence bag.

"That's a curious set of photos," Branden said. "It's curious that they're here."

Wilsher shrugged, not quite sure what to make of them at

the moment. In the bathroom, they found broken glass bottles, a shattered mirror over the sink, and lotions, liquid soaps, and what was left of aftershaves splattered on the walls and in the toilet. On the floor they found a white powder scattered around a crushed brown plastic prescription bottle. Branden lifted the cracked plastic bottle with Wilsher's pen and managed to straighten the curled label enough that they could read the contents, *Lithobid, 300 mg.* Wilsher used a business card to shovel some of the powder into a bag and said, "If he wasn't taking his lithium, there's no telling what he's been like the last couple of weeks."

In the shower stall, Branden found an uncrushed tablet, and Wilsher bagged that too. The floor of the shower stall was stained dark brown from rust in the water, and the shower head had been forcefully bent up at a sharp angle so that it couldn't be used, even if the water were turned on. Branden opened the cold water valve, and there was gurgling and hissing before a burst of brown water sprayed out of the bent shower head, onto the ceiling.

Ricky Niell, at the computer table, called them back into the living room and displayed a letter on the screen. Branden and Wilsher bent over to read, and discovered it to be an early letter to Weaver, saying Yoder knew what Weaver was up to, by the surveying he had been doing for Weston. The letter carried a stern warning against dividing up the land of Yoder's relatives.

Another file with a later date repeated the warning. Ricky had opened four files in total, but Branden asked about the one that was in the printer's out-tray. Ricky nodded and switched from the hard drive to a disk in drive A. There he clicked on "Untitled-1," and the letter in question appeared on the screen. "He's got an automatic 'save' when a file is closed," Ricky said.

Branden bent lower and took the mouse. He clicked on *Summary Info* under the *File* menu, and then chose *Statistics*. The *Created* line displayed the date, 11:17 A.M., and the revision number was 1. Under *Last Printed,* it read 11:19 A.M. Branden performed the same tasks for the other letters and found the next most recent letter to have been dated almost two weeks earlier than the one in the printer's tray.

Wilsher said, "I'm going to need printouts of all those letters, with their statistics," and Niell squared up to the keyboard and began working. Wilsher led Branden out to the carport.

The deputy had finished fingerprinting the trunk and was now working inside the cab, on the steering wheel and the door panels. Wilsher walked slowly up to the car and said, "I'm glad you didn't see her, Mike. She's been here a while, and with the heat . . . "

"She was a good friend, Dan, thanks."

"The guys took her out real careful. She was puffy from the heat, but it looked to me as if she'd been strangled. There was a line of deep bruising all around her throat."

"Call Missy," Branden said. "Get a time of death."

"She knows to call me as soon as she has it, Mike."

"It's important. Larry Yoder has been in the hospital since late afternoon last Thursday."

"He could have done this as easy as anyone. Set fire to her house, too," Wilsher said.

"The timing is not gonna fit."

"How do you figure that?"

"Last week, Yoder should have been depressed and drunk, not manic."

"Those drawings are as manic as they come, Mike."

"We don't know when they were done."

"Don't know when Britta was murdered, either," Wilsher said.

Branden shrugged and let the matter drop. "Is there anything else here, Dan? Behind the trailer?"

Branden started around the carport, and Wilsher followed, saying, "There's junk piled out back."

Deputy Armbruster appeared from around the back corner of the trailer, holding up a stick. Mounted on its end was a dirty, faded, rubber mask, a goat's head with horns.

Wilsher took the stick and held up the mask, frowning with disgust. "Yoder's tied in with everything, it seems."

Branden stepped close and studied the mask on the end of the stick. "This is an old one, Dan. Could have been from long ago."

"Or well used," Wilsher countered.

"It also could have been planted here, like anything else. The rifle. Those cartridges."

Wilsher handed the mask on the stick to Armbruster and said, "That goes in, along with everything else. Don't shake it any more than you have to."

Armbruster nodded and headed for the front of the trailer.

Said Wilsher, "That does it for me, Mike. Yoder's our man. The mask ties in with Ricky's shed, and the mask robberies go all the way back to J. R. Weaver. I figure he did Sommers too, because of the land swindles."

"That's too easy, Dan," Branden replied.

"It's as easy as that, because it's as simple as that."

"Yoder's parents never mentioned anything about the occult. They would have known."

"Maybe he got out of it a while back, Mike."

Branden turned toward the back of the trailer and said, "More likely, it was planted by someone who knew Yoder well."

Wilsher followed, saying, "I'm still going to give it to the captain that Yoder did it all."

"Give it more time, Dan," Branden encouraged.

Wilsher shrugged and followed Branden to the rear of the trailer.

Behind the trailer, near the woods, there was an overturned black charcoal grill, its four rusted legs up in the air. Several garbage cans were stuffed to overflowing, and one had tipped over and spilled out its reeking contents. A stack of weathered lumber leaned against the back of the trailer, and a battered lawnmower was parked nearby. A dirt bike lay in the dust on its side, at the head of a trail that led into the woods.

Branden lifted the bike onto its wheels and unscrewed the gas-tank lid. He rocked the bike back and forth and heard gasoline sloshing inside. He screwed on the lid, mounted the bike, and kicked down on the starter several times. Soon he had the engine growling and crackling as he worked the throttle back and forth, and he popped the clutch and whirled several doughnuts into the dried grass. He shut the engine off and said, "Had one of these as a kid."

Wilsher laughed and shook his head. "There's more to do inside."

Branden said, "I'm going to follow a hunch about this trail," and restarted the bike. Wilsher turned toward the trailer, and Branden took the bike into the woods.

The trail rose east and crested on a knoll behind Yoder's trailer. From there it descended sharply into a ravine and crossed a dry stream bed. Up again on the other side, it let out into a high pasture of brown grass and clover. It skirted the pasture along the tree line and circled around to the north, where it followed a ridge for several hundred yards. Eventually, the trail began a slow descent through stands of pine and oak, to a low point where a blackened field edged Route 515. Across the burnt field, for almost a hundred yards, Branden had an unobstructed view of the spot on 515 where Weaver had turned his buggy into his driveway for the last time.

27

Monday, August 14
8:35 P.M.

"I FOUND the place," Branden said to Taggert, "where Yoder waited to take his shot at Weaver. And a dirt bike to get him there and back."

Missy wasn't paying attention. Robertson lay on his back in the burn unit at Akron Children's Hospital, eyes closed in the dim room.

"Please don't wake him up," Missy said, and left.

Branden kept vigil at Robertson's bedside for nearly an hour before the sheriff spoke.

"It's still hot outside?"

Branden nodded. "Upper nineties for the most part."

"What about the fire at Britta's house?"

"That's all set up to look like Yoder did it. Killing Britta, too."

"Doesn't sound like you buy it."

"Not completely," Branden said. "It looks as if he would have had the time to kill Britta. But in his state of mind, after shooting Weaver's horse, I don't see it."

"Why?"

"Can't say for sure, Bruce. But it's too much to do. For Yoder, I mean. Try to kill Weaver, and hit the horse instead. Then strangle Sommers, and burn her house up. I don't see Yoder having the wherewithal to do that before he showed up at his parents' house Thursday afternoon."

"Then how 'bout," Robertson said and halted. He waved his hand weakly, squeezed his eyes closed to think, and said, "You know. Britta's ex. Dobrowski."

"He's a wife beater, Bruce, and therefore a coward. Hasn't got the stones to kill anyone."

"We ought to check on it anyway."

"Let me see what Bobby's doing about it," Branden said half-heartedly and studied the sheriff's face.

Robertson's eyes closed, and Branden said into the room, "I'm working on it, Sheriff."

Later, in a whisper, Robertson said, "You were right about Missy."

"I'm glad to see you've finally caught on."

"I think I've always liked her. Figured it was respect. You know, the girl who can do everything. But it's more, Mike." He shifted awkwardly on his back and groaned softly.

"You've been thinking about her for a long time," Branden offered.

"Can't think of anything else," Robertson said, labored. "When she's here, I feel like I can handle anything. When she's gone, I feel like a radio program with a long stretch of dead air."

Branden nodded and watched the sheriff.

Robertson squeezed his eyes shut, and whispered, "I want you to get me a new pair of cowboy boots, Mike."

"Boots?"

"Yeah. Dancing boots. Go over to my place and get that old pair out of my closet."

"Cowboy boots?"

"They're in the closet in my bedroom. Stuffed way in the back."

"Then what?"

"I want you to get me a new pair just like 'em. Smooth ostrich skin. Twelve and a half, extra wide. I like Dan Posts. They used to have them down at Trail's End, just north of Delaware on Route 23."

"OK, I can do that," Branden said, and waited.

Sadly, Robertson said, "Renie and I used to go country-western dancing a lot. There's a nice little dance hall over by Brewster—The Red Lantern Barn. It has a good wooden floor, and they give lessons through the week. Then you go there on Saturday nights for the big dances."

"You're gonna take Taggert dancing?"

"I'm going to ask Missy to start taking lessons with me."

"A date."

"More than one."

"People will talk," Branden teased, worried about the sheriff's state of mind.

"Don't care, Mike. No one has made me feel like this since Renie died. No one but Missy."

"All you want me to do is get your boots?"

"No. There's more. I want you to find out what size Missy wears and buy her a matching pair."

"Then what?"

"Get them wrapped, Mike. Bows, ribbons, everything. Before I leave this hospital, I want to give them to her as a present."

"Before you leave."

"I'm gonna do that, Mike."

"I know. What makes you think Missy will take up western dance?"

"Missy can do just about anything, Mike."

"But what makes you think she will *want* to?"

"You just get the boots, buddy. Let me handle the rest."

28

Tuesday, August 15
9:20 A.M.

"HE'S GOT a trail, Bobby," Branden said to Captain Newell in the sheriff's office at the old red brick jail. He held up an empty coffee cup at the credenza, and Newell waved him ahead. Branden poured a cup, walked across the big room to Robertson's desk, and sat in front of it, in a straight-backed, gray metal office chair.

Newell waited behind the big desk for additional information, but Branden sat quietly, taking little sips of the hot brew.

Newell asked, "How about the dirt bike Wilsher said you rode?"

"Took it down the trail behind Yoder's trailer. It led straight to J. R. Weaver's farm. Yoder had an ideal position for rifle work."

"That's all we're gonna need, Mike. We're charging Yoder with everything. Weaver, Schrauzer, and the others. Britta Sommers, too."

"I told Dan I wasn't sure about Britta," Branden said, uneasy.

"He had means, motive, and opportunity."

Branden appeared unconvinced.

"Missy Taggert says Sommers died of strangulation sometime early Thursday morning," Newell said. "Yoder wasn't on his way to the hospital in Canton until late that afternoon."

Branden said, "I'm working on a different angle."

"We've got the letter Yoder intended to send to Weaver after he shot up his buggy."

"Anyone could have produced that letter," Branden said. "Could have reset the date on his computer in order to make it appear that the letters had been written before Weaver died."

Ellie Troyer appeared in the doorway and ushered in a man and a woman, announcing them. "Captain Newell, this is Mr. and Mrs. Smith. Parents of Brad Smith."

Newell came out from behind his desk and greeted them, shaking their hands. Branden rose and said, "I hope you've had some luck with Bill Keplar."

Lenora Smith crossed the room to Branden and took up his hand in both of hers. "We have, Professor. Thank you!"

She turned back to Newell and said, "We've hired a PI, Captain, and you're going to be surprised by how much we have learned about the crash that killed our son."

Newell seated them in chairs in front of his desk. Branden stood at the left side, and Newell sat behind the desk and asked, "A PI, Mr. Smith?"

"Please, it's Denny. And yes. We've hired a private investigator in Chicago to look into the truck driver and his company. We know why our son died, and we know who's going to pay for it." He turned to Branden and added, formally, "Thanks to Professor Branden here."

Newell gave a curious glance toward Branden and asked, "Can we lay charges against the driver?"

"It's not just the driver," Mr. Smith said.

Ellie Troyer's voice came softly over the intercom. "A gentleman to see you, Captain."

"Can it wait?"

"It'd be better if you came out, now."

Newell pushed his muscular frame out of Robertson's chair and said, "I'll be back."

Branden rose to refill his coffee cup and poured one cup each for the Smiths. They sat quietly in their chairs and waited with the mugs in their laps. Branden lingered by one of the tall office windows and squinted into the glare of bright morning sun. He pulled the shades and drank his coffee, remembering dim, watered, forest glens—cool, quiet, and peaceful.

Through the thin paneled wall, they heard a raising of voices. Branden recognized Arden Dobrowski's. He set his coffee cup down beside the coffee maker on the credenza, turned to the Smiths, said, "I still want to hear what you've got for the captain," and went down the hall to Ellie's front counter.

Dobrowski scowled bitterly and said, "I want that man locked up," pointing a finger at Branden.

Newell said, "You're not pressing charges, remember, Dobrowski?"

"I've changed my mind."

Branden started purposefully through the counter's swinging door, but Newell clamped both of his hands on Branden's shoulders and hauled him back.

Branden wrestled free of the captain's grip and stood where Newell had planted him. "Don't go anywhere, Dobrowski," Branden said. "You're a suspect in Britta's murder."

Dobrowski guffawed. "Get real, Branden. I've lost a tooth on account of you."

"You've got a bad habit of not listening, Dobrowski. You're a suspect. Don't leave town."

Dobrowski whirled around and stomped out of the jail.

Ellie asked, "Did he just press charges against the professor?"

"Not that I heard," Newell replied. He stiffened next to the counter, flexed the taut muscles in his arms and shoulders, and demanded, "What was that all about, Mike?"

"Dobrowski and I don't get along."

"I can see that," Newell said. "Now tell me why."

Branden hesitated with a scowl on his face, and Newell repeated, "Tell me why, Mike."

Heated, Branden said, "About a month before Britta divorced him, she called me out to her place. When I got there, she was bruised, had a black eye, and her lip was split. I stayed with her a while, and Dobrowski came back. Even with me there, he started in on her again. He was drunk and abusive and took several swings at her. I had to lay him out. That's when Britta started talking about divorcing him."

"And what was that about Dobrowski's being a suspect?"

"Somehow Dobrowski's gonna benefit from Britta's death. An insurance policy. Something in her will. She always took out partner's insurance, one for the other, in business affairs."

"So?"

"Britta owned most of Dobrowski's auto dealerships at one time. Dobrowski's probably still got a policy on her."

"Nevertheless, you're gonna let me decide who is a suspect and who isn't," Newell said officiously.

Branden shrugged, and said, "I was just giving him something to think about. Besides, he could have framed Yoder for Sommers easily enough."

Newell stepped wearily back into the sheriff's office, saying, "This is a simple case, Mike. You're thinking too hard again."

Branden smiled wanly and took a seat beside the sheriff's desk. He nodded to the Smiths and said, "You'll be interested in the answer to this question." Turning to Newell, he asked, "What did Jimmy Weston bring you yesterday that got you that warrant so fast?"

Out at Ellie's counter, there was a commotion, and just as Robert Cravely pushed through the sheriff's office door, Ellie spoke over the intercom, "Sorry, Bobby. He wouldn't wait."

Cravely bounded into the office, dropped his heavy briefcase onto the floor, and began wiping sweat from his face with a crumpled and stained handkerchief.

Newell sat rigidly behind the desk, neither acknowledging Cravely nor letting his disapproval of the little man show on his face. Branden watched Cravely and realized the insurance agent had not recognized the Smiths.

Cravely took a stance with his feet planted wide and, ignoring the professor and the Smiths, challenged, "I know you've got bullets and a rifle from Yoder's trailer that will exonerate my driver."

The captain said nothing.

Cravely knelt and opened his briefcase on the floor. When he had pushed himself up, he held a document of several pages, bound in a black clamp folder. "This is my final report," he said, and tossed the document onto the sheriff's desk.

Newell glanced at it, but didn't pick it up. "I don't care what you've got there, Cravely. We're charging your driver with a DUI, multiple vehicular homicides, depraved indifference, whatever. I've just come from Phil Schrauzer's funeral, and I can promise you this. You're gonna pay off Schrauzer's widow. Robertson's medical bills, too, and the parents of the boy who died out there!" He cautioned the Smiths with a glance, and they sat tight. Denny Smith's face was flushed a brilliant red, and Lenora Smith had a death grip on the arms of the chair. "Whatever Larry Yoder might have done, your driver put that truck into a jackknife because he was drunk, not because Yoder shot a horse!"

Cravely snorted. "Yoder killed more than those people, Captain. I know about Ms. Sommers."

Branden sat up straighter to say something, but Newell cut him off. "Maybe Yoder did kill Britta Sommers. That doesn't let you off the hook for the others."

"Yoder killed everyone," Cravely snapped and bent to lift his briefcase. "You have my report."

Denny Smith rose slowly from his chair, fists clenched at his sides, and turned to face the insurance agent. Taking hold of the small man by his lapels, he boosted Cravely violently off his feet and pushed him back against the office wall where Robertson's collection of police arm patches was displayed. Cravely squirmed, and a handful of patches fell from the wall behind him.

Newell managed to take Smith from the back, pulling his grip on Cravely loose. Pushing Smith away, Newell stepped around to put himself between the two men.

Cravely yelped, "You rotten cur!" and Smith lunged again at the man. Newell held Smith back, the muscles in his neck and arms straining his uniform.

"That's enough, Smith," Newell said, and pushed the angry man back into his chair.

Lenora Smith sat quietly weeping. Denny Smith got up again and stood behind her chair, holding her shoulders. He looked angrily at Cravely and started talking in a forced, yet soft tone, laced with bitter animosity.

"We know the whole story, Mr. Cravely. None of it, I am quite sure, will be found in that report of yours.

"You see, we hired a detective in Chicago, and we know all about your company and that driver who killed our son. That man has been fired once before. For drunk driving, Cravely. He's had a history of DUIs, and he crashed another of the company's trucks last year. So they fired him. But what do you know! The regular driver was out sick last week, and your company rehired the bastard because they didn't have anyone else to make the run.

"Well, he made the run, all right. Stopped off in Wooster to have a few cold ones. The bartender there has recognized his picture. Then he showed up drunk at his first stop, and the Amish carpenter remembers trying to sober the guy up with coffee. Tried to stall him. Keep him from driving.

"But, no! Your guy had to get back in that truck. He was drunk, Cravely, before he crested that hill, and it's your company who's to blame. I don't care what's in your report. Nothing about our son's death is settled. Not to my way of thinking."

Smith scowled at Cravely for another half minute and then helped his wife out of her chair, and they left.

Cravely's face was flushed red. He made a pretense of straightening his suit coat, and bent to pick up his briefcase. Then he turned sharply and stomped out of the room.

Branden shook his head. He picked up Cravely's report in the black binder, flipped some pages and set it down. With a new sense of urgency, he asked the captain again, "What did Weston give you that secured the search warrant?"

Newell refocused his thoughts with an effort. "What?" he eventually said to Branden.

"You said Weston came in here yesterday and told you something new to help get a search warrant for Yoder's place. What was that?"

Newell thought for a moment. "He told us Larry Yoder had told him all about shooting Weaver's horse. Back when Weston took him out to his parents' house on Thursday afternoon."

Branden shifted in his chair. "Why'd he wait this long to tell you that?"

"I don't know. He said he didn't take it seriously at first, knowing Yoder as he did. But then he had just heard we were trying for a search warrant and thought maybe he could help."

Branden remembered a small detail from the accident scene and observed, "This whole thing is starting to make some sense to me, Bobby. Do you have Ricky Niell's notes from the accident?"

Newell rose and walked out to Ellie's radio consoles. "See if you can raise Niell," he said. "Ask him where his notes are on the Weaver accident."

Back in the office, Newell found Branden sitting on the edge of his chair, hands cradling his forehead. Soon Ellie had an answer and retrieved Niell's notebook from a file drawer in the squad room. She carried it into the sheriff's office and laid it on the desk. As she stood there, Branden roused from his thoughts, looked around, and saw Niell's spiral notebook. Newell handed it to him, and Branden said, "Thanks," distantly.

"You've figured something out?" Newell inquired.

Branden shrugged, said, "Maybe," and left the captain sitting at his desk.

As he paged through Ricky Niell's notebook, Branden walked the block and a half north to the *Holmes Gazette*. He asked to see Nancy Blain, was directed to the second floor, and found her coming out of a back room. As she came forward, Branden said, "Nancy, I need your help."

Blain motioned him to her black metal desk, next to a bank of matching file cabinets. She took a seat at the desk, and Branden said, standing, "I remember your taking photographs at the accident the day J. R. Weaver was killed."

She nodded.

"I'd like to borrow those prints for the afternoon."

Blain said, "I never thanked you for what you did for Eric last year."

Branden remembered the tranquil summer afternoon when they had talked about Eric Bromfield, while she took photos of an Amish valley.

Her hair was still short. She was dressed in brown leather walking shoes, jeans, and a simple white blouse. She took off a pair of glasses and dropped them into the center desk drawer, saying, "OSHA doesn't let you wear contacts in darkrooms anymore," and added, "Thanks for Eric, Professor."

Branden said, "I'm glad I was of some help," and "I'll only need them for a few hours."

Blain turned to the file cabinet nearest to her desk. From the second drawer, she drew several folders of six-by-nine prints, and laid them on her desk for the professor. "They're all numbered, but try to keep them in order anyway."

Branden tucked the folders under his left arm, shook her hand, and said, "Thanks."

"You'll bring them back today?" she asked.

"I might need them until tomorrow, but I doubt it. Probably later this afternoon."

Blain said, "OK," and Branden headed for his car, leafing through the photos as he walked. Halfway through the stack, he spotted one photo in particular, and stopped beside his car to study it, a shot of a dull yellow Ford F150 pickup, with its windows rolled down and a splinter of wood with tatters of ripped black cloth lying across the windshield. Branden eased in behind the wheel, laid the photos on the passenger's seat of his car, noted the number on the back of the photo, and wrote in a spiral notebook: *Photo 28—Windows Down.*

At his house, Branden dropped Blain's photographs on the kitchen table and checked the one phone message indicated on his answering machine. It was Ricky Niell, saying, "Doc, the captain asked me to give you an update: I checked on Dobrowski. He was sleeping off an all-night drunk in the Wayne County Jail when Sommers's house was torched. I called Wooster to verify that, so he's got an alibi."

Branden deleted the message, sat down with the photos, and flipped through the little spiral book, laying out certain photos when they matched Niell's account. He became more anxious each time he read Niell's notes from the accident scene and from the interviews with MacAfee, Weston, and Kent. And then he had it. The whole of it, wrapped up neatly with a bow.

The phone rang, and he rose slowly from the table and answered it.

"Mike, this is Henry DiSalvo."

Branden didn't speak at first.

"The will, Mike."

"Weaver's?"

"Right. I'm going to read it Wednesday morning. Only two people are to be present. Andy Weaver and one witness of his choosing. Other relatives are to be informed by post."

"Strange," Branden said and glanced back at the photos spread out on the kitchen table. "Say, I don't think I'll need that appointment at 11:00 A.M., but why couldn't you read the will earlier?"

DiSalvo chuckled. "Weaver had stipulated that I was to wait to see which of his relatives would inquire about his money. All of them have, now, except Andy Weaver. He alone has made no inquiries whatsoever."

Back at the kitchen table, Branden slowly closed Ricky Niell's notes, and put Blain's photos back in order. He smiled, rapped his knuckles on the tabletop, and sat down with his arms folded over his chest. One person's movements had given it away. Even the motive was there, plainly in view all along. It only remained to verify certain facts. To discover how things were done, and when.

29

ON THE stretch of 515 that runs in front of Weaver's house, Branden pulled his car onto the right berm facing north, and turned his hazard flashers on. He opened Ricky Niell's notebook and again read the entries for the first interviews with MacAfee, Weston, and Kent. Then he flipped back to the second interviews, read them slowly and wrote: *First Interviews!* in his spiral notebook.

By reference to photos 26 through 29, Branden was able to back his sedan precisely to the spot where the yellow truck had stopped at the time of the accident. He rolled his windows down and sat listening. Over the crest of the hill just beyond Weaver's drive, he saw a brief puff of black smoke. A semi crested the hill, came down past Weaver's drive, and went by in the oncoming lane. Branden wrote *Schrauzer!*— on a line in his notebook.

He turned his gaze left and studied the burned field on the other side of the road. At the far edge of the field, he could see the break in the trees where Yoder's trail came out of the woods. In his notebook he wrote: *Yoder in plain view.*

Branden pushed all of the photos he had used back into their folders and stacked the folders on the floor, where they'd be less likely to slide around. Then he started his engine, pulled forward on the road, and turned left into Weaver's drive. As he made the turn, he saw another belch of diesel smoke over the hill. He watched in his rearview mirror, and a semi passed by on the road behind him. On the line where he had written *Schrauzer!—* he added *SMOKE*.

Branden parked his car in the drive, walked around to the back of the house, and tried the door to Weaver's study. It was locked. He took out a credit card, worked it into the slot between door and frame, at the point where the latch would be, and pushed. The latch gave, and the door opened. He closed it, and in his notebook he wrote: *Yoder got at the rifle easily enough.*

Back in front, Branden stood at the end of Weaver's drive, on the spot where the horse had fallen beside the road. He found a clear line of sight to Yoder's shooting position across the field. *Line of shot unobstructed.*

At Yoder's trailer, under the carport, Branden found a new red plastic gas container in plain sight. He checked at the back of the house and found two rusted metal gas cans lined up beside the skirting on the trailer. The cans appeared to be about the same vintage as the mower that stood nearby. He returned to the front, and put the new gas container in the bed of his pickup.

He came down Yoder's gravel drive, drove up the hill to Walnut Creek, went through town past the restaurant and the Inn, and took Rt. 39 back to Millersburg. There he found that Missy Taggert had gone to the hospital in Akron. He left the gas can on her autopsy table and wrote a note asking that she compare the residue in the can with the samples Niell had collected at the fire scene.

While still at Pomerene Hospital, the professor made two calls, one to Holmes Estates in Cleveland, and one to the hospital in Dover.

At Britta Sommers's place, Branden parked beside the brick ranch house and walked onto the back patio. Shards of glass were cast about on the flagstones. A line of yellow spray paint marked the run of blackened stone where a gasoline fuse had burnt toward Sommers's back door. Near the woods, about thirty yards from the house, a yellow circle had been painted on the grass to mark the origin of the fuse. On his hands and knees, Branden felt delicately in the grass and soon found other slivers of window glass. A spar stuck in his palm, and as he worked to remove it, he got up and turned to inspect the trunk of the nearest tree. He saw that it, too, had been peppered with flying glass. In his notebook, he entered: *Too short a fuse*.

Inside the house, it appeared that nothing had been touched. The place was still a cluttered mess, even where the fire hadn't reached. Branden tried unsuccessfully to match this image with the meticulous office Britta had kept. *Signs of a search*. With this written, he stepped back through the rubble in the kitchen and noted the place in the study where someone had pulled papers out of Britta's files and made a point of burning them separately. *Needed to destroy files* went into his notebook.

Outside again, Branden took his pocketknife and began working one of the larger pieces of glass from the trunk of a tree. With his back turned to the house, he heard the metallic clicks and snappings of a lever-action rifle being chambered and cocked. Without surprise, he turned slowly to see Jimmy Weston pointing a carbine at his chest.

"Figured you wouldn't let it be," Weston said. "What gave me away?"

"Backfires, Jimmy," Branden said pointedly.

"I don't get it," Weston said.

"You didn't tell Ricky Niell you heard a backfire the first time he talked to you out at Weaver's accident."

"That's all?"

"Your windows were down, Jimmy."

"Air conditioner's on the fritz."

"You, most of all, should have heard the shot. I figure you

heard it well enough, and probably saw Yoder, too, over by the trees."

Weston nodded grimly. "It took a couple of minutes to figure the whole thing out. Murder Britta, frame Yoder, and all. But I reasoned that when the deputy came around again, I should tell him I heard a backfire just like everyone else."

"That phone call, supposedly from the Dover hospital. That was weak," Branden commented.

"Got cut up with the explosion," Weston said. "What else could I do?"

"You should have left Britta alone in the first place!" Branden shot.

"You're the only one who knows about any of this, Branden."

"I've turned in everything I have to the sheriff's office," Branden proclaimed.

"Sure you have, Professor. How could I expect anything less? But I won't be around long enough for that to matter."

"I wrote it all down, Jimmy. Gave it to Captain Newell. I'm surprised he hasn't arrested you by now."

"You're bluffing."

"I am not, Jimmy."

"So let's hear it," Weston challenged.

"OK. Monday. You got to Yoder early in the evening. Kept him drunk for the next couple of days. Drunk and off his lithium. You, if anyone, would have known what that would do to him, as unpredictable as he was on the job. Tuesday you'll have made one last try, talking Britta out of it. That didn't work, so Wednesday night, you killed her at her home. Or maybe it was early Thursday morning.

"Next, you set fire to her house, drove her body to Yoder's, and planted her in his trunk and the gas can in his carport. You also arranged some things for us at the trailer, like the rifle and 30-06 cartridges we found. Probably those hunting photos in a dresser drawer, too. I'll bet you even typed the letter we found in Yoder's printer. Then you drove Yoder to his parents' house, ostensibly because you were worried about him.

"Friday, you made a point of calling Becker. It was just good fortune that I was there when he took that call. But that cemented your alibi for the cuts on your face. Then you sat tight.

"But by Monday, you couldn't take the pressure anymore, so you gave Newell that tip. Got us a warrant for Yoder's home. Does that about cover it, Weston?"

Weston was agitated. He circled around behind Branden, jammed the muzzle of the rifle between his shoulder blades, and pushed the professor down the slope, onto the back patio, and around to the side driveway where Branden's car was parked beside the house.

"Open your trunk, Professor."

Branden took keys out of his jeans pocket, unlocked the trunk, and slowly lifted the lid.

Holding himself several paces back, Weston said, "Now get inside and toss me the keys."

Branden complied, dropped the keys on the ground near the bumper, and waited, kneeling in the bottom of his trunk.

"Lie down with your back to me," Weston commanded.

"You're not going to get away with this, Jimmy."

"Lie down, Professor, and shut up."

Once Branden was curled up with his back to the rear, Weston came forward slowly, holding the rifle on Branden. He bent quickly to pick up the keys, reached up with his left hand, and slammed the trunk lid shut.

His voice muffled from inside the trunk, Branden shouted, "I wrote it all down for Bobby Newell, Weston. You're not helping yourself any," and immediately began the slow task of turning himself around inside the small trunk.

"You just hang tight, Professor. I've got to figure out what to do with you."

Weston ran down the curving drive to his battered yellow

truck and hauled himself up into the cab, then slumped momentarily behind the wheel, exhausted from the week of watching,
waiting, and guiding the investigation toward Yoder. Just now,
with the professor, he had been calm. Murder was easier the
second time around. Or maybe, he thought, he was just numb.
Probably that. Numb since the day Britta had told him she was
selling him out to Holmes Estates. Numb with humiliation and
the disgrace of losing his business.

In Millersburg, he stopped in the alley behind his office building and took a red gasoline can out of the garage behind the
Victorian house. At a filling station, he used a credit card at the
pump, so that he would not have to go in to pay for gas. And
as he drove back through town, the magnitude of his problems
seemed to rush hotly into his mind, confounding his thoughts,
overwhelming his emotions. This was instinct, now. A plodding,
mechanical fixation on being free of it all. As irreversible as a
plunge off a cliff.

His eyes fixed on the pavement in front of him as he drove,
and he began to curse Britta Sommers out loud. To curse the
days in high school when they had dated. To curse her for mar-
rying Arden Dobrowski. To curse her for buying into Weston
Surveying to keep his business going. To curse her for letting
Holmes Estates force him out. And, crying silently, to curse her
for not understanding in time that he would have to kill her.
That she had left him no choice.

On Route 62 outside of town, he dried his eyes and traveled
east to Britta's driveway. He felt detached from his actions as
his growling diesel truck crawled back up the winding drive to
Sommers's house. He backed slowly into the stand of pines
near the house, and pulled forward, pointing the nose of the
truck down the drive. He left the engine running, lifted the can
of gasoline out of the bed of his truck, and screwed on the white
flexible spout as he walked back to Branden's car.

Starting at the trunk and working methodically forward, he

splashed gasoline over Branden's car and on the ground surrounding it. When he had finished at the front hood, some gas remained in his can, and this he poured out under the trunk of the car and in a line that descended the driveway to a point near his diesel, some twenty yards away.

He put the empty gas can back in the bed of his truck, reached into the cab, and took out a box of kitchen matches. He held three together and dragged the heads across the striker plate on the box until they caught. Then he tossed the burning matches onto the end of the gasoline fuse.

The fire leaped along the fuse quickly, reached the car, and erupted, with a loud whoosh, into a giant ball of orange and yellow flame. The flash of the ignition forced Weston backward with his arm thrown over his eyes. He crouched, shielding his eyes, and hurried around to the front of his truck, protected, now, to a certain extent, from the heat.

When he drew himself up straight and opened his eyes, he found himself staring down the barrel of Branden's .38 revolver.

Branden cocked the hammer with his gun hand, and held a pair of handcuffs out in his left, saying, "One would think, Jimmy, that you'd have learned your lesson about pouring too short a fuse."

30

ANDY Weaver descended the narrow steps from Henry Di-Salvo's law office ahead of Cal Troyer. The Dutchman stepped out onto the sidewalk with the pastor and blinked in the bright morning sun. He popped his straw hat on his head, studied the sidewalk for a moment, and frowned.

Cal slapped him on the back and asked, "What are you going to do?"

Weaver shook his head slowly from side to side. "It is a great lot of money, Cal," he said.

"You have to think of this as an opportunity," Cal said.

"Temptation, Cal," Weaver replied softly. He cast his eyes down the sidewalk and stared for several minutes. "Do you ever think about quitting?"

"Preaching? No," Cal answered.

"I'm tired, Cal. Weary to the bone."

"Find a way to make this money work for good, Andy."

"It's too much money for one man," Weaver said and then seemed to stir from a dream. "Can you come out to the house tomorrow morning? I need to think."

Cal said, "Sure," and watched the bishop turn and walk slowly toward the courthouse.

When Weaver reached the light at Clay and Jackson, Cal crossed the street and pushed through the thick walnut doors of Hotel Millersburg. He walked down the long, quiet hallway and found Branden at a table outside in the little courtyard.

Branden had an iced tea, and Cal ordered the same when the waitress appeared. The octagonal picnic table was set in the shade of an old maple tree. Branden leaned forward on his elbows, with calm satisfaction.

When his tea arrived, Cal squeezed lemon into the glass and asked, "You knew your gun was in the trunk?"

"Of course," Branden said, smiling. "Do you think I'd have let Weston stuff me in there otherwise?"

"And you got out how?"

"Screwdriver. Took about a whole minute."

"Ellie says you brought him in with cuffs on and then spent more than an hour writing out your conclusions for Newell."

"I wouldn't say it took an hour."

"Ellie timed it at an hour and ten minutes."

Branden grinned and thought of Ellie out at the front counter, watching the clock. "I had a lot to write."

"About Weston?"

"Right. His actions over the last week or so, plus his means, motive, and opportunities. The trail he left."

The waitress returned, took their orders without writing, and ambled back inside to the kitchen.

"What about your session just now with DiSalvo?" Branden asked.

"The will?"

"Right. Why did DiSalvo have to wait this long to read the will?"

"J. R. Weaver had an opening statement. Said his relatives were all hypocrites and the only one who deserved his money would be the one who had never wanted it in the first place. DiSalvo was to give it to the last relative who inquired about an inheritance."

"Andy Weaver," Branden whispered, amazed.

"He gets it all," Cal said. "Never planned on asking for any of it."

"Just how rich is he?" Branden asked.

"Eleven and a half million, once you cash in all of the stocks and bonds, and pay the taxes."

Branden whistled. "That's the last you'll see of Bishop Andy R. Weaver."

"Not Andy Weaver," Cal said and smiled with confidence.

"He's got nothing in his district but trouble. You said so yourself."

"Andy Weaver has got visions of building a church, Mike, not a fortune," Cal said.

"That's more temptation than any man could withstand."

"His brother had a problem with greed," Cal said. "Not Andy. He hasn't even decided whether or not he'll accept the money."

"At the very least, that's the kind of money that could give him a fresh start somewhere else," Branden said.

"He'll stick with the church," Cal said confidently. "If anything, he'll consider this to be tainted money. Might not even want it."

Branden rubbed at his chin and laughed. "Eleven-plus million, and J. R. Weaver couldn't even give it away."

"I'm going out to see Andy tomorrow," Cal said. "I expect he'll have made up his mind by then."

The food arrived, and Branden took an eager bite of a club sandwich.

Cal had a soup and salad. Eyeing Branden, he said, "Now it's your turn. Give it up, Professor."

"You mean Weston?"

Cal nodded and started in on his salad. "When did you first suspect him?"

"He made a lot of mistakes, Cal."

"But what was the first one?"

"The first one I caught onto was the flying glass from the explosion at Britta's house. I knew we were looking for someone who was all cut up. But the first mistake he actually made was not reporting a backfire at the crash scene when he was first interviewed."

They ate quietly together, enjoying the shade on the patio. Branden finished before Cal, and as he pushed his plate forward on the table, he asked, "What did you and Andy accomplish up at Holmes Estates last Monday?"

As he ate the last of his soup, Cal said, "Andy tried several ploys. First, he asked them to sell the land back to him outright."

"That wasn't going to happen," Branden said.

"I don't think he expected it to," Cal said. "Next, he offered to sell them two farms in place of two others. So that the two families who planned to stay in the area could have the better land. That didn't work, either."

"Would Weaver have gone for that one if they had agreed?"

"I think so. But I think what he really wanted was the last proposal he made."

Branden waved the waitress over for more tea, and stirred in sugar when she brought it. "And that was . . . ," he prompted.

"He offered to sell Holmes Estates the eight farmhouses and five-acre tracts that Weaver hadn't already sold them. That gave Holmes Estates unbroken stretches of land where the eight farms stand."

"That I'll bet they went for," Branden said.

"Of course. But Weaver said he'd have to check with his families, added that the price would have to be right, and left them there to think about it."

"So, he's decided to move the whole lot of them somewhere else," Branden said. "Do you know where?"

"He has letters out to settlements in several western states," Cal said.

"I'd sure like to see that, Cal. All those families with their goods piled in buggies and wagons. A convoy at five miles an hour, headed west."

31

CAL and Andy Weaver turned into the front drive at the Ader
Mast farm in Weaver's plain black buggy. Weaver pulled to a
stop before they reached the house and stared ahead with a
look of absolute resolve. Cal sat quietly beside him, nervously
considering what Weaver was about to do.

Cal pointed to the slope in front of the barn doors, and there
sat two buggies with their horses. The barn door was slid open
about two feet, and they could hear horses inside, kicking
against their stalls, stamping the dirt, and whinnying nervously.
Ader Mast Senior appeared on the front porch of his house,
waved them down to the barn, and hurried back inside.

Weaver parked his buggy near the doors to the barn and
stepped down. Despite the heat, Weaver was dressed in full black
Sunday costume. Cal remained on the buggy seat. He held the
scriptures under one arm and observed Weaver expectantly.

Weaver glanced up to Cal and whispered, "Pray, Cal. While
I have a go at it. Watch for tricks, but pray! We must be very
stern."

Cal nodded his determination and said, "I've already started."

Inside, Weaver found the two fathers, Homer Yost and David
Yoder, standing apprehensively beside the first stall. With them
were Weaver's two preachers, Wayne Hershberger and Ben
Yoder. With a severe expression and stiff posture, Weaver ap-

184

proached the preachers and said in dialect, "For the unity of the Church, we must put a stop to this here and now. Cal Troyer is outside and will assist me if I need it." He saw the sting of his reproach register in the preachers' eyes, and figured it was warranted.

To the fathers he said, with authority, "If your sons return to us, you'll instruct them every day about the Evil One. It is necessary, and you will be watched. I will talk with the boys once each week for many months to come."

Both fathers nodded vigorously, frightened and very much chastened.

Weaver took the preachers gently aside and, with his eyes cast down because he was embarrassed for the men, he said, "This is where Melvin P. failed. There have been a few boys for several years involved in this. Larry Yoder was one of the first, and he is in the nut house. How could you not have known?"

The one answered, "We are praying, Bischoff. We should have done something."

"You must not fail to preach against this."

"We will not fail, Bischoff."

"Then kneel, now, and pray, Ben. Pray, Wayne, as you have never done before. Pray for the unity and safety of the Church. For peace. For the souls of these two boys. If the Lord does not bless us now, we are lost."

As the preachers knelt in the straw, Weaver cast his eyes around in the dim light and asked, "The boys?"

The preacher Wayne cleared his throat and stammered, "In the back."

Weaver peered into the far corner of the barn and saw two lads talking together in the shadows. He took several paces toward them, but turned back to the fathers and said, "Wait outside, please. Pray for your sons."

Both men shuffled their feet but held to their places, and Weaver intoned, "Go now! Wait outside. When I come out you'll either have your sons back, or, you'd better believe it, they'll be lost to us for good."

When they had left, Weaver whispered gruffly to his preachers, "We wouldn't be in this mess if those two had been proper fathers."

The men winced at the bishop's uncharacteristic sternness and watched Weaver march into the back regions of the barn.

32

BRANDEN cruised into the parking lot across the street from Akron Children's Hospital and tapped lightly on the boot box that lay on the seat beside him. He inspected the wrapping paper, light green with glitter, and straightened the bright yellow ribbon and bow. A corner of the wrapping paper had lifted up, and he took a tape dispenser off the dash of his truck and taped the paper down again. He got out under dark afternoon skies and hurried to the elevators in the corner of the parking lot, shielding the package from the light mist and rain that was developing, as the outriders of an approaching storm broke the long summer drought.

In the glass and steel archway over Bowery Street, he stopped to watch the clouds. The pelting mist soon turned to a blowing rain that glanced along the window, streamed down, and puddled and flowed toward the storm drains on the street below. A nurse in white opened the outside door from the parking lot, and as she entered, Branden felt the moist coolness of the late summer storm as the skies darkened considerably and the rain strengthened to a steady, thundering downpour. A sense of belonging, connectedness, affirmed his woodland instincts.

He lingered on the crossway until the rain slackened to a light drizzle. As he watched the steam rising off the blacktop below, he set his package down, took out his cell phone, and with his optimism restored, he called Dr. Waverly at the psych ward in Aultman Hospital in Canton. He learned only that Yoder was making slow progress toward understanding what he had done to J. R. Weaver.

Branden closed the phone, dropped it into his shirt pocket, took up his package, and negotiated the turns and interior corridors of the hospital until he arrived at the burn unit. At the reception counter on the left, he inquired about Robertson and asked for a yellow paper gown, cap, and face mask.

"Dr. Taggert is still in Robertson's room," she said. "Been there almost all day."

"Is it OK if I go on back?" Branden asked.

"No more than two at a time," she said. "I'll let them know you're coming."

The nurse keyed him through the main door to the burn unit, and circled back to the counter to use the intercom.

In Robertson's room, Branden found the same battery of pumps and monitors against the wall behind the sheriff's bed. The lights in the room were dim, and Missy Taggert sat in her yellow gown and mask in a large and heavily padded brown upholstered hospital chair with a tall, straight back.

She turned to Branden and said, softly, "We've just changed his bandages."

Branden laid the green and yellow package on the foot of Robertson's bed, and the sheriff came around, eyed the package, and griped, "I guess that's the best color scheme one can expect from a college professor."

The professor smiled for Robertson's benefit and exchanged glances with Taggert. She shook her head sadly.

The intercom crackled, and a nurse announced that Deputy Ricky Niell was waiting outside to see the sheriff.

Missy pushed out of the big hospital chair and said, "I'll step out." Quietly, she drew the professor aside and whispered, "He needs encouragement, Mike. Some reason to hang on."

When she had cleared the room, Robertson pushed himself up with effort and asked, "Are those Missy's boots?"

"Smooth ostrich skin, just like you said. Had to back-order your size, though."

Robertson nodded, and eased back on his pillows.

"Does it hurt much?" Branden asked.

Robertson shrugged. "Mostly it wears you out."

Niell came into the room in a yellow paper suit and said, "Do we have to wear these masks all of the time?"

Robertson waved Niell to his bedside and, struggling, said, "Newell says you figured out who was robbing buggies, and found their hideout."

"It was a ritual barn," Niell said. "Satanic. We tore it down yesterday. The party who owns the land gave us permission. He didn't even know it was there."

Robertson's expression coaxed more, and Niell added, "The owner lives in Cleveland. Hasn't actually been on the property in ten years."

"But you did catch the kids who were doing it?" Robertson asked.

"Not really. All I know is what Bishop Weaver told me this morning. All the people who were robbed have been paid back personally by two kids from his congregation."

"So Weaver knows who was doing it," Robertson concluded. "We can get their names."

"Weaver won't give them up," said Niell.

Robertson shook his head side to side.

Branden said, "That's going to be a dead end, Bruce," and Robertson seemed to accept it.

"Now tell me how you grabbed up Weston," Robertson said to Branden, rising up with effort onto his elbows.

Branden started to explain about being locked in his trunk, and Robertson cut him off. "No. I mean how did you figure him out?"

Branden took a seat in Missy's large brown chair and said, "When I was looking through Ricky's notes from the accident, I remembered something that had seemed curious when I first heard it from Ricky in the emergency room."

Robertson held his eyes closed and waved his hand for more.

Niell said, "At first, Weston didn't report that he had heard a truck backfire."

"Right," Branden said. "And he, most of all, should have heard one. His air conditioner was broken and all of his windows were down. Besides, MacAfee's produce truck was brand new and wouldn't have had any engine problems."

"But Weston did report hearing a backfire in my second interview," Niell said.

"Took him a while to realize he needed to have heard one," Robertson offered in a whisper, and lay back with his eyes closed.

"He saw Yoder with Weaver's rifle," Branden said. "His truck was parked in just the right place to see back toward the woods. He would have heard the shot, seen Yoder, and eventually figured out that he had to report hearing a backfire like all the others. That would give him time to frame Yoder, because even then he intended to murder Britta. Probably got the idea right there at the accident, if he wasn't already thinking about it before. Then he made two cell phone calls from the accident scene. One was to his partner, Becker. The other one is going to turn out to have been to Britta."

"Why?" Robertson asked.

"Britta was selling out, Bruce. Everything. Right down to her majority share in Weston Surveying. Weston had sold her sixty percent a few years back just to keep afloat, and he knew Holmes Estates would call that due as soon as she had sold it to them. His phone call was one last try to convince Britta not to sell him out, with Weaver dead. When she refused, he started planning to murder her, framing Yoder."

"Why would he do that if she was already determined to sell?" Robertson asked softly.

"Partner's insurance," Branden said. "They had $250,000 policies on each other. If she died before finishing the sale to Holmes Estates, Weston could at least walk away with that. Plus the sale of Weston Surveying would be less likely to go through."

"That's all speculation," Niell said. "What proof do you have that he actually did it?"

"Flying glass," Branden said, obviously satisfied with himself. He waited to let Robertson and Niell think about it.

"At the fire at Britta's house, he poured too short a fuse. I found shards of window glass back as far as the tree line. His face and hands got cut up pretty badly, so the next thing I heard from him, through Becker, was that he had gotten scratched on a job site over near Dover. Trouble was, the Dover hospital has no record of his being there, and when I called Holmes Estates, they remembered Weston having been up there the day he was supposed to have been cut by brambles and a rusty barbed-wire fence."

"So he called Becker from Cleveland to give himself an alibi for the cuts he got when he torched Britta's house," Niell concluded.

"And to hide the fact that he was really up in Cleveland trying to save his company," Branden said. "You see, the key was to get to Yoder fast, probably as early as Monday afternoon after the crash, and keep him drunk and off his medicine. Well, Yoder was pretty far gone by then anyway, and when Weston took him to his parents' house last Thursday afternoon, Yoder was totally incapable of saying anything coherent."

Niell said, "OK. You saw that all in my notes about the backfires. But when did you first suspect Weston?"

"When Becker took Weston's call. It was the cuts. I knew we

were looking for someone whose face was cut by flying glass. It was just too convenient for Weston to have gotten cut on the job where no one could have seen him."

Niell continued. "Why did Weston come in so late to tell Newell that Yoder had confessed that he had shot Weaver's horse? You would think he would have come in earlier."

Robertson listened with his eyes open again, as Branden explained. "He was just slow to think it through. He needed us to get out to Yoder's trailer faster. Had it all set up for us. Not just Britta's body, but inside the trailer, too. The letter in the printer. Crushed Lithobid tablets on the bathroom floor. The cartridges from the rifle and the gas can. He was slow to figure he needed to nudge us Yoder's way, so we'd find where he had planted Britta's body. In truth, he should have waited for us to find Britta ourselves, as we eventually would have done."

"Weston planned the whole thing," Niell said.

"From the moment he saw Yoder with that rifle at the accident scene," Branden said.

"There's a lot of dumb mistakes, there," Robertson said and pushed gently with his hands to move himself up onto the pillows. He failed and lay quiet, breathing hard.

"Over-management was Weston's principal mistake," Niell said. "If he had just sat tight, we might never have got him."

The intercom carried the nurse's voice from the front counter. "Pastor Troyer would like to come back."

Niell fiddled with his yellow mask and said, "I've had about as much of this mask as I can take."

He left, and soon Troyer appeared in his own yellow cap and gown. As he entered the room, he said, "I've got Andy Weaver waiting outside," and "Do you all know it's raining?"

Robertson seemed pleased and smiled. "Is it going to do any good?"

"Looks like a steady, all-day rain," Cal said.

Branden asked, "Visiting Holmes Estates, Cal?"

Cal laughed heartily. "You'll never believe what he has pulled off."

Robertson asked, "Who's that, Cal?"

"The new bishop in Melvin Yoder's district."

"Tried to buy his land back?" Branden asked.

"Didn't just try, Mike. He actually did it."

"So he's not moving, after all?" Branden asked.

Cal nodded. "He went in there with an offer already in mind. Had it all planned out."

"Buy what land?" Robertson asked.

"J. R. Weaver swindled eight of his district's families out of their farms," Branden said. "Ultimately, that's what got him killed." To Cal he added, "How'd Andy pull it off?"

"He told them he had 8.5 million in inheritance from Weaver's estate. Offered it all to them for the eight farms they had bought from Weaver. Convinced them that they'd be better off making a quick profit all around than fighting it out in court for several years."

"That was obviously a bluff," Branden smiled. "Amish'd never take Holmes Estates to court."

Cal said, "Exactly," with great satisfaction.

"What's he plan to do with the rest? I'm sure he didn't mention the full eleven and a half."

"He says he's going to use the rest to establish a fund to pay real estate taxes for everyone in his district, every year, forever, and use some portion of the principal to buy as much land as he can, even at inflated prices."

Robertson asked, "Why not just keep all the money?"

Branden answered. "Money is nothing to them. Land is everything."

"He could move anywhere he wanted on 8.5 million," Bruce said.

"I asked him about that," Cal said. "He said something like, 'Our troubles are not with the location of our hearts. Our troubles are with the devils in our hearts. So how would moving somewhere else solve our problems?'"

Robertson seemed to rouse a bit and said, "I still can't believe he'd spend 8.5 million just to stay where he is!"

Cal lifted his arms, palms up, and asked, "What's a peasant farmer going to do with that kind of money, if he hasn't got his land?"

Branden changed the subject. "What about those two boys Ricky says are paying off on those robberies?"

Cal said, "Andy Weaver had a little talk with them yesterday," and shook his head. "When he came out of the barn with them, they had just been shaved. Weaver had them both by the back of the collar and handed them over to their fathers like they were going to toe the line, or else."

Robertson grumbled, "Humph," and asked Branden, "How about Larry Yoder, Mike?"

"I just phoned his doctor. He's making progress. Seems to want to talk. Maybe we'll know someday if he meant to kill Weaver or just scare him. But the psychiatrist also hinted at something untoward in Yoder's life."

"Something like Satanism?" Robertson asked.

Cal held his peace.

Branden shrugged.

"Then that leaves just one thing," Robertson said. "How did Phil Schrauzer know, ahead of time, to try to back away from that crash?" His eyes fluttered and closed.

"A puff of black smoke, Sheriff," Branden answered. "When you park on 515, about where Phil was stopped that afternoon, you can see diesel exhaust when semis downshift coming over that rise. Phil saw the exhaust before the semi hit the crest. He also saw Weaver's horse falter and knew there wouldn't be time for Weaver to clear the road."

Robertson shook his head, saddened. "Phil deserved better than that."

A silent moment passed and Missy came back into the room. "It's time the sheriff had a rest, boys."

"Just one more thing, Missy," Cal said. Smiling, he asked, "When's Caroline coming home, Professor?"

"I'm flying out there, tomorrow," Branden said, instantly on guard.

"That doesn't give you much time," Robertson grinned, catching Troyer's eye.

"The sheriff's right, Mike," Cal needled. "You'd better start cleaning now."

"I wouldn't know what you're talking about," Branden said, unconcerned.

"I'll bet the dishes alone are enough to cook your goose," Robertson whispered.

"You all underestimate me," Branden smiled.

"I took pizza over to his place the other night," Cal said to Robertson. "House was a mess."

"I'll have you both know the house is spotless," Branden said.

"Then you've hired it done," Cal challenged.

"Three Amish sisters," Branden said, celebrating.

"Now you've just got to stay out of the place till then," Robertson laughed, and then coughed heavily, wincing in pain.

"All right, then," Cal teased. "Why are you flying to Arizona?"

Branden smiled broadly. "Caroline bought a new, two-seater sports car. A Miata. We're going to drive it home with the top down, before classes start."

Cal stood up and walked out, laughing. They could still hear him out in the hall as he left.

Robertson poked his toe at the package lying at his feet and whispered, "Hand me that box before you go, Mike."

With Branden gone too, Robertson pushed weakly on the

boot box beside him on the bed, and said, "This is for you, Missy." He looked at her and thought she seemed genuinely surprised. Perhaps bewildered.

"Just open it," Robertson whispered.

When Missy took the boots out of the box, her expression was of delight mixed with awkward embarrassment. She didn't speak, but set the boots on the bed beside the sheriff, waiting.

Robertson reached for her hand and said, "Missy, without you, I'm as useless as a train ticket to Aruba."

Missy began to cry.

Softly, Robertson pleaded, "Don't cry, Missy. Please don't cry."

She popped a tissue from a box on top of one of the regulators and dried her eyes as best she could.

"Let's go dancing, Missy," Robertson breathed. "Lessons on Thursday nights. Dances on Saturdays."

"Line dancing?" she asked, clearing her throat with difficulty.

"Cowboys don't line dance," Robertson said. "This would be couples progressive dance. Country-western."

Missy drew near to him and spoke softly with flowing tears, as one hand brushed lightly over his short gray hair. "I hear you and Irene Cotton used to do that," she whispered.

Robertson pulled her hand closer and managed only to say, "You and me Missy. I'm hanging on. Just you and me."

The next book in the Amish-Country Mystery Series

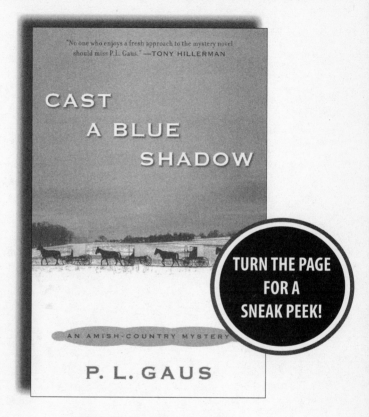

ISBN 978-0-452-29669-5

www.plgaus.com

Available wherever books are sold.

Plume
A member of Penguin Group (USA) Inc.
www.penguin.com

1

Saturday, November 2
Dawn, Holmes County, Ohio

CURLED up in her black down parka, Martha Lehman lay on her side, back pressed firmly against the polished wood door, knees drawn tightly to her chest. The white block lettering on the door read Dr. Evelyn White Carson, Psychiatrist. Martha was aware only of the rough, cold carpet pressing into her cheek and of long, ragged breaths that repeatedly dragged her out of a trance. Thus, for an hour, before sunrise bled pink hues through the window at the end of the second-floor hall, she lay in a stupor, hounded again by a dreadful loneliness.

In wakeful moments, with a fervor born of an all-too-familiar pain, she renewed a childhood vow. Silence, she thought, had never betrayed her, and it was Silence she'd cling to now. Silence had brought her to Dr. Carson as a child, and Silence she would trust again. Then, it had been Carson who had understood the wordlessness. The sorrow and isolation of a mute child. It will be Carson, now, she prayed, who will remember.

Thoughts formed only intermittently, in a cold, tortured nightmare of helplessness.

Silence again, she vowed—now, more than ever before. The snap and pop of blue cotton shirts and black denim vests in a stiff winter breeze, clutching at her from a clothesline.

Alone again, and safe that way. Menacing, cracked lips that sternly mouthed, "Save your little sisters." A childhood nightmare, empowered, somehow, to hurt her again.

How had She known? A man's blue shirt tore loose from the clothesline, enveloped her face, and smothered her, its weight unbearable, its odor a familiar horror. On weak child's legs, she struggled to carry the burden of an adult, and managed to breathe only in gasps.

Too soon for Her to have known it. And yet She had. The wind began to whisper judgment from the clothesline. Shirt sleeves snapping near her eyes. Wagging fingers, all of them.

Fallen like Babylon, Martha Lehman. "So, choose, young Martha," an urgent voice pleaded. "Choose the better way."

Sonny, what have you done? The frowning congregation walked out of the barn, all their faces down, all their backs turned. No one dared to believe it possible. To accept the hell it signified.

What plans now? He's lost to you. No place for plain girls in his murderous world. Nor any place in the old. No haven for outcast girls.

The cold tracks of tears on her cheeks slowly awakened her. She unclasped her knees and felt a binding stickiness between her fingers. Unzipping her parka, she instinctively pressed her palms to her belly and felt the stickiness there, too. Sitting up, she brushed hair from her eyes, smearing her forehead. She looked down in confusion and saw her white lace apron stained dark red. Gasping, she fell back on her side, knotting her fingers into the bloody fabric.

Vaguely, now, she recalled brief snatches of last night's disastrous conversation with Sonny's mother. She dimly remembered driving away in the snow. A sleepless night of confusion and frustration. Her decision to go back. The blood. Running. Fleeing in the storm.

But these were indistinct memories. Perhaps more dreams, she thought, as she lay motionless. Mere impressions. As if her mind had conjured events that her heart could not allow.